PUFFIN BOOKS

MY FATHER is NOT a COMEDIAN!

I wrote this book. It's about me. And my father, of course.

Anyway, it wasn't even my fault – the comedian thing. It was just something I said to a reporter from a newspaper.

But then someone started following my father. Someone I didn't trust. So I took matters into my own hands.

Well, I had to protect my poor father.

Somehow, it wasn't as easy as I thought.

Claudia

Also by
Ursula Dubosarsky

High Hopes
Zizzy Zing
The Last Week in December
The White Guinea-Pig
The First Book of Samuel
Bruno and the Crumhorn
Black Sails, White Sails
The Strange Adventures of Isador Brown
(an Aussie Bite, illustrated by
Paty Marshall-Stace)
Honey and Bear
(Illustrated by Ron Brooks)

MY FATHER is NOT a COMEDIAN!

URSULA DUBOSARSKY

PUFFIN BOOKS

This book is dedicated with great gratitude
and affection to the Arnold family.
Thank you!

Puffin Books
Penguin Books Australia Ltd
487 Maroondah Highway, PO Box 257
Ringwood, Victoria, 3134, Australia
Penguin Books Ltd
Harmondsworth, Middlesex, England
Penguin Putnam Inc.
375 Hudson Street, New York, New York 10014, USA
Penguin Books Canada Limited
10 Alcorn Avenue, Toronto, Ontario, Canada, M4V 3B2
Penguin Books (N.Z.) Ltd
Cnr Rosedale and Airborne Roads, Albany, Auckland, New Zealand
Penguin Books (South Africa) (Pty) Ltd
4 Pallinghurst Road, Parktown 2193, South Africa

First published by Penguin Books Australia 1999
1 3 5 7 9 10 8 6 4 2
Copyright © Ursula Dubosarsky 1999

Designed by Nikki Townsend, Penguin Design Studio
Cover illustration: Nigel Buchanan
Typeset in Aldus Roman 11.5/16 pt by Midland Typesetters, Maryborough, Victoria
Made and printed in Australia by Australian Print Group, Maryborough, Victoria

National Library of Australia
Cataloguing-in-Publication data:

Dubosarsky, Ursula, 1961- .
My father is not a comedian.
ISBN 0 14 130208 9.

I. title.
A823.3

note to the reader

I wrote this book. It's about me. If you're wondering why I wrote a book all about myself, I have to tell you I had it on VERY GOOD ADVICE that you should write from LIFE. So this is it.

In case you're also wondering why I put some words in capital letters, this is to make sure you don't MISS them. Also, I sometimes put capitals for hard words that you might not know, to make it easier for you to look them up in the dictionary.

I have to put some hard words in because I want to become a Baroness. You can be made a Baroness for 'Services to Literature' and that means you have to use hard words.

I don't know why I want to become a Baroness.
It's my ambition, that's all. First I wanted to
be a tight-rope walker, now I want to be a
Baroness. That's it. I'm very stubborn.

Yours sincerely,

Claudia

Claudia (Baroness) (one day) XXX

chapter one

I BEHAVE VERY NOBLY . . .

My father is not a comedian. It's true, it was in the paper. It was only the local paper, but enough people saw it to make my father look at me in a despairing kind of way and say, 'Why? Why, Claudie, why?'

My name is actually Claudia, after the Emperor Claudius of Ancient Rome, who was weak and misshapen and walked with a limp. Well, he was weak and misshapen on the television, anyway. There's a series about him called 'I, Claudius'. There are twenty-seven parts with about three hundred poisonings and murders and many more terrible things from which you should Avert Your Eyes.

Anyway, it wasn't my fault – the comedian thing. What happened was this: A reporter and a photographer from the local newspaper came to our school in the week before Father's Day. Our teacher said, 'Children, these people have come to talk to you about Father's Day. Who would like to tell this nice man all about their father?'

How would she know he was a nice man? But she's always saying how everyone's nice somewhere in some little part of them, and that you have to encourage it.

'We've been doing lots of lovely things for Father's Day this year, haven't we, children?' said our teacher firmly to us.

Well, if you call a lovely thing making spiders on sticks out of old egg cartons, which is the sort of thing five-year-olds do. But our teacher is used to teaching kindergarten, this is her first year teaching anyone as old and bad as us and I think she keeps forgetting where she is.

Abigail put up her hand because she's the tallest and she's been in the local paper before for making a life-size chess set out of papier-mâché. It took her about a year to make, and she gave every piece a different face and painted them and even put clothes on them. She has to keep them in the backyard, because they won't all fit in her bedroom and her mother won't let her put them in the living room because she said they gave her a bad feeling in the middle of the night. I think it was a bit unreasonable, because out in the garden they got wet and soggy and now hardly any of them are standing up any more and they just look like lumps of mouldy old newspaper.

Anyway, Abigail's used to publicity, so that's why she put up her hand and said, 'My father is a Member of Parliament,' which was one big lie but when I asked her afterwards she said that lying was the secret to publicity, and she should know.

Maybe the reporter suspected or maybe he wasn't that interested in Members of Parliament, because he just said in a bored kind of way (as though every class he'd spoken to had at least half a dozen fathers who were Members of Parliament), 'Yeah. Okay. Anyone else?'

Abigail sat down rather grumpily but then Anupam put up her hand, stood up and said, 'My father is a specialist in soil.'

Well, I never knew that and I looked around at Anupam to see if she was lying too but she seemed perfectly composed.

'Ah!' said the reporter, getting excited (well, a little). 'So, does he travel around the country much?'

Why would he do that – to inspect lumps of dirt?

'No,' replied Anupam serenely. 'He sits all day in an earthy chamber.'

Well, only Anupam would say something as peculiar as that, and everyone laughed, even the ones who were half asleep and hadn't even noticed there were visitors in the classroom.

Then Alaric put up his hand. Alaric is a beautiful round boy with fair hair that's quite long and people always think he's a girl and sometimes even his mother forgets and says things like, 'Oh are you looking for Alaric, I think she's on the swings.' Alaric doesn't mind what people think he is, boy or girl – he thinks it's funny, and he's my favourite boy at the moment but I'm pretty fussy so he'd better be careful.

Alaric said, 'My father's in the cemetery and we go to visit him on his birthday and we sit on his gravestone and eat sandwiches and there are always these big lizards there, looking at us with beady eyes.'

That's the sort of thing you can see Alaric and his mother doing – if you met them, you'd know what I mean – and I think it sounds very interesting, just what you might want to read in the paper, but the reporter rolled his eyes and said to our teacher, 'I'm hoping for something a little more upbeat than a graveyard.'

This wasn't exactly very sensitive, and our teacher who thinks everyone's got the teeniest tiniest bit of niceness in them, (that's how they think in kindergarten) looked AGHAST, but then she bit her lip (which she's always doing) and she called upon one of her Old Faithfuls.

'Cinnamon!' she said briskly. (Yes, there really is a girl in our class called Cinnamon, but her sister's not called Nutmeg, she's called Alice which is not fair at all. We call Cinnamon 'Sin' for short, meaning a bad deed, which she can do when she wants to.)

Cinnamon stood up and looked very fresh and photographable. She said, 'My father is an English High School teacher, and he is Beloved Far and Wide.'

She said Be-lov-ed like they do in weddings, which is what she actually meant because her father has been married three times and his three wives all live very far and wide from each other.

6

The reporter shook his head and muttered something to the photographer – I suppose he thought Cinnamon was some kind of maniac, and she is, actually. So our teacher, getting desperate, called upon her other Old Faithful, Leo. He is a godly boy who wants to be a priest. He would be a nice priest, because he has curly hair which is the best look for that kind of occupation.

Leo stood up and smiled with his lovely clean cheeks. He is very pale because he's not allowed out in the sun, like a vampire.

'My father is unemployed,' Leo began – he has a deep fruity voice which he copies from coffee advertisements on the radio.

The reporter nodded enthusiastically – I suppose this was what he was looking for – something that would give him a chance to write about economics because that's all they write about in the papers it seems to me. Not that I read them much, but our teacher makes us cut out the headlines every week and pin them up on a cork board, so you can't help noticing things. Well, some people can, half the people in my class don't seem to notice anything at all, but it's always been one of my problems, noticing things.

'Lost his job, did he?' asked the reporter cheerfully, and the photographer started preparing the apparatus, but Leo said, 'He's retired, actually. He's eighty-two years old.'

Well, now our teacher looked FLABBERGASTED, and well she might because Leo's mother is certainly not eighty-two years old, she's just about the most glamorous mother in the school and she always wears golden high-heeled shoes, even to school sports days, where she regularly gets stuck in the mud. Now we understood why she never brings Leo's father along – he's probably in a wheelchair or about to have a heart attack and nobody wants a death at a sports carnival, do they? We all stared at Leo. Imagine having a father that old! He must have had Leo when he was seventy!

'Boaz?' said our teacher, quickly moving on because I don't think she wanted to hear any more about Leo's eighty-two-year-old father.

Boaz stood up. Boaz's father is famous, we all know about Boaz's father.

'My father's a comedian,' he mumbled, looking down at the desk, because Boaz is a very embarrassable sort of person and he blushes a lot.

'Ah,' said the reporter. 'Okay. Now that's interesting. Tell us a bit about it.'

Boaz mumbled again. He hates talking about his father. He's only interested in rubber bands. He has the biggest collection in the school, which he keeps under his desk. If you lift up the desk, it looks like an infestation of very thin worms.

'Well, where does he perform?' asked the reporter.

'IN A PUB!' shouted Boaz suddenly, which is one of his odd little habits. I suppose we're all used to it by now, but the reporter jumped on the spot like he was in the army, and dropped his pencil.

'Look, I think we might try another class,' he murmured *sotto voce* (this is Italian for 'in a soft voice', which is what our Italian teacher, Signora Biltorina, is always screaming at us).

That's when I behaved very nobly, for all the thanks it got me. Our teacher looked so sad as if she was about to burst into tears, which she does from time to time, when 'it's just all too much for me, all too much . . .' And well, anyway, I'm a nice person – let's face it, I notice things – so I jumped up out of my seat and called out to the reporter, not trying to be funny or anything but just encouraging because Boaz had shouted at him so loudly.

'My father is not a comedian!'

Well, even the reporter laughed then, and our teacher stemmed the flow of tears, sniffing them back bravely, and the reporter nodded to the photographer and said, 'This one'll do,' and then he said to me, 'Well?'

'Um,' I said.

Now I was in a bit of a fix. My father is not a comedian, but what exactly is he? There were quite a few things I could say about him, but most of them shouldn't end up in a newspaper. In the end I picked the one I'd heard him use himself, he couldn't complain about that.

'My father's a spaceman!' I said, and the flash of the camera lit up the whole room.

chapter two

... WHICH MAKES ME FAMOUS BUT GETS ME
INTO TROUBLE AT HOME ...

So there it was, in the local newspaper, a photograph of
me looking positively depressed and the great big headline
MY FATHER IS NOT A COMEDIAN. And there was
my father at the end of my bed with his bowl of vile
porridge and the newspaper in his hand, eyeing me like
a reproachful labrador and saying, 'Why? Why, Claudie,
why?'

'I didn't know it'd turn out like that!' I said from
under the blankets, closing my eyes tight. That's something I often find myself saying.

'Oh, oh, oh!' cried my father, but he left the room
before I could try to explain, not that I was going to. He
probably went onto the balcony to do some deep breathing.
My father's an Engaged Buddhist, and Engaged Buddhists
take lots of deep breaths, I believe.

I opened my eyes and came out from under. He'd left the newspaper on the floor. I took a quick look at it, and then a little bit longer look, and a bit longer still. Then I stretched out in bed, picked up the paper and had a lovely long stare at myself.

As I said, I looked very gloomy in the photograph, but that's just my natural expression. How was I supposed to know he was going to take the photo right then? Before I had a chance to put on the beam I keep for public occasions, like when I'm in charge of the pony rides at the school fete and none of the little children want to get on.

There wasn't much in the article, just a few lines under the headline, saying:

'Her father may not be a comedian, but she'll still be celebrating Father's Day on Sunday. Despite high levels of unemployment and further drops in interest rates . . .'

Well, I wasn't going to waste my time reading that. On and on it went, without a mention of my name! What was my father complaining about?

The reporter hadn't even put in the bit about my father being a spaceman. This was probably because he didn't believe me, but it's true. Sort of true. He's a kind of a spaceman. Not the kind who wears a helmet and silver foil suit and goes up in a space station and plays golf on the moon. He's a different kind – the kind that sells SPACE – that's a spaceman, isn't it? He sells space, and anything else he can.

At the moment though, my father's not selling anything at all. He stays at home all day. He's not exactly unemployed; he's in hiding. This happens from time to time, when things get out of hand. It's a jungle out there, he says to me mournfully, lying on the sofa in front of the television.

Business is like that; sometimes people aren't very satisfied with the results. When that happens, my father stays inside for a few weeks until things settle down and the people outside with the pieces of paper and the big sticks have got sick of waiting. I'm not going to go into business when I leave school. It's too dangerous, although I suppose it would be interesting to claw my way to the top.

'CLAUDIE!!!!!!!'

That's my little sister, Griselda. What a terrible name – lucky it wasn't me. It means 'patient wife'. She's mad. When she was a baby, she wanted to be a guinea-pig. She used to get right inside the cage and eat their leftovers. That's mad, there's no two ways about it.

'CLAUDIE!!!!'

She doesn't do that any more because both our guinea-pigs died in a mysterious plague – anyway, now she's too big for the cage.

'CLAUDIE!!! CAN I COME IN???'

That's her. Wherever you are – wherever anyone is, guinea-pigs included – she wants to come in. When she gets in, she doesn't do anything, she just *bes*. But she knows she has to knock if it's my room, or else I grab her round the neck and show her my teeth and she gets scared. She's six years old, but very easy to scare.

'NO!!' I shouted back.

'But I'm a human being!'

Dad taught her to say that – what do I care?

'GO AWAY!'

'But I'm STARVING to death!' wailed Griselda.

She's always like that – never hungry or thirsty or tired, always starving to death, dying of thirst, or exhausted. She's very passionate, I suppose. My parents are both very passionate too. But I'm not passionate, I'm a nice person.

'Go away,' I repeated, dropping my voice to a sinister whisper, and that terrified her of course, so she scuttled away to our mother. She and our mother are the best of friends – they are both interested in seeds. They sit on the sofa together reading seed catalogues. I am not interested in seeds. Not at all.

I ripped out the sheet of newspaper with my photo on it and stuck it up on my wardrobe door with glue, over the top of a picture of a mouse that Griselda stickytaped over the top of my abstract collage and she knows perfectly well we're not allowed to stick things on the furniture.

I lay on my bed happily looking at my photograph. I thought that soon I had better start a scrapbook, like Abigail. She keeps a scrapbook of all her 'clippings' (that's what they call them in the publicity business). She's got the photo of her with the lifesize chess pieces and the birth announcement that her parents put in the paper when she was born. That's all she's got, so far.

'CLAUDIE! WE HAVE TO GO TO SCHOOL!'

'ALL RIGHT!'

Luckily I forgot to put on my pajamas the night before so I was all dressed in yesterday's school clothes. It saves a lot of time, you know, if you wear your clothes to bed. I pulled my school bag out from under the bed and went over and unlocked the door. Griselda tumbled in and ran over to get her bag. She sleeps in the same room as me, but it's definitely MY room. Everything belongs to the eldest child, it's called the law of PRIMOGENITURE. I found this very good word in the dictionary. Anyway, in she came, wiping wet Cornflakes everywhere. No one else I know insists on eating Cornflakes with their fingers. She's mad.

My father was still on the balcony taking deep breaths when Griselda and I left for school, so I suppose he was still grumpy about the newspaper article. In my opinion he shouldn't go out on the balcony, just in case one of those people who are looking for him has a slingshot or something worse. But it wasn't the moment to mention it, so I just called out, 'GOODBYE THEN!' and slammed the door.

As we walked to school I saw that all the letterboxes of the houses we passed had copies of the local newspaper sticking out. I felt rather warm thinking how everyone would be looking at my picture.

'I'm famous,' I said to Griselda, who was sucking on her plait. Griselda is a very oral person.

'I'm FREEZING!' replied Griselda. 'I'm DYING of the cold.'

Griselda's teacher told my parents that Griselda has 'a highly developed sense of grievance', adding that it might be useful in later life. They meant, I suppose, that it wasn't that useful right now . . .

At school, Alaric was hanging on the front fence, grinning. 'I saw your picture in the paper!' he called out. 'My mum said you looked disturbed.'

'Maybe I am,' I said, with a shrug. I had to expect jealousy, after all.

I went over to the fence. Whenever I get near Alaric, I want to give him a hug. He's very cuddly. This is because of all his SUBCUTANEOUS fat – well, that's what he says. People are always trying to cuddle him. Once our teacher, who is used to the kindergarten where they go in for that sort of thing, actually gave him a cuddle but he said, 'Please don't. You're invading my personal space.'

Alaric says lots of things like that because he sees a psychologist every two weeks. His mother makes him go, ever since his father died. Actually, it was the psychologist, I found out, who came up with the idea of eating sandwiches in the graveyard, and if you ask me, that psychologist should see a psychiatrist.

Anyway, I restrained myself from cuddling Alaric and instead we dug a hole and put a pile of pebbles inside it.

Leo came over and looked at it and said, 'Is that an altar for a sacrifice?' which probably sounds a bit weird but remember, Leo has God on the brain.

chapter three

. . . I EXPERIENCE A CREATIVE STORM . . .

After the bell went and we all trooped inside the classroom, I was pleased to see that our teacher had pinned a copy of my picture and the article underneath it on the corkboard. Everybody, I'm afraid, was making unpleasant remarks about it – well, everybody who was awake, that is, which was about three people. Our teacher said, 'Hush now, children. Let's see if we can hear a pin drop!'

You have to feel sorry for her, don't you?

Pretty soon our poor teacher gave up trying to hear a pin drop and she clapped her hands above her head instead. Teachers learn to do these things at teacher school – Cinnamon told us. But her dad always says, 'I'm waiting till they bring back the cane!' How could such a man be married three times? But Cinnamon says he's very satirical, and when we asked her what that meant she frowned and said, 'I think it means he's half a goat, half a person,' which makes it all the more amazing that he's been married three times, if you think about it.

Anyway, I smiled encouragingly at our teacher, because I'm nice and I'm very sensitive to the sufferings of others, all the good it does me.

Our teacher was standing at the front with a tall tower of dictionaries on her desk. 'There's a dictionary for every member of the class!' she said, smiling brightly. 'Isn't that a wonderful thing!'

Well, that's a bit of a deep question for my class, who are better at answering things like, 'Who has brought their lunch money?' or 'Is is cold outside?'.

Anupam and I sit in the middle of the room. This is a strategic choice, because our teacher either looks at the front, where Leo and Cinnamon sit and they are always doing their work, or she looks right up the back where Ethelred is, who is never doing his work. She likes extremes, I suppose, like Griselda. If you sit in the middle she never notices what you do one way or the other.

Our teacher said, 'Now, everyone PAY ATTENTION!' and she banged her hand on top of the tower of dictionaries and they all fell on the floor in a great tumble of noisy words and everyone, even Ethelred, who was woken up at last by the crash and probably thought it was an earthquake, ran to the front to help pick them up.

Then we all had a dictionary in our hands and we went and sat down again and looked at our teacher.

'Right. Well done, class. Now what we are going to do today is play the Dictionary Game!' Our teacher loves games. 'To learn through play' – she says it's a quote from a famous person, although I think the famous person might have been talking about babies at the time.

'What I want you to do,' she went on courageously, 'is open up the dictionary and find the strangest word you've ever seen.'

Our poor teacher. In the kindergarten you could do something like that without danger although I don't suppose anyone in kindergarten can read. But in our class anyone could have told you that certain elements (I mean, certain people – 'elements' is what you call them when you want to be insulting) – were only going to find certain sorts of words that our teacher wouldn't want to hear about at all. Anyway, she seemed to notice this happening quite quickly for her, and she made a new rule to the game. She wrote up on the board in very big letters:

'NO OBSCENITIES' and when Boaz said, 'What's obscenities?' she said (rather smartly, I thought), 'Look it up in the dictionary.'

I flipped through the dictionary. I like dictionaries. I like the way they have very dark inky writing and then very pale grey inky writing. And I like all the bits in italics and the bits in brackets. (I like brackets, as you may have noticed.)

'I've got a word!' called out Leo, and Cinnamon looked furious because they are always in a competition over who can finish their work first and get extra work to do.

'Good boy, Leo,' said our teacher, 'but don't say what

19

it is, please. I need to give you some more instructions for the game.'

'I've got a word,' said Anupam to me, but very softly because she didn't want Cinnamon to get angry with her as well, because Cinnamon looks sweet but she is an expert at giving Chinese burns.

I looked over to where Anupam held the dictionary open, her finger at the top of the page. 'Dappled'.

Dappled! 'What's so strange about that!' I said scornfully, because Anupam and I like to be honest with each other. At least I do. Anupam just looked gracious and said, 'It's strange to me,' and you can't argue with that, I suppose.

I flipped the pages over and over and back again. There were so many words I didn't know, it was daunting. I wondered if a Baroness would be expected to know all the words in the dictionary? Embrocate, sneezewort, ophiology . . .

'Children,' said our teacher, 'if you've all found a word . . .'

'Is hinterland a strange word?' asked Alaric, forgetting to put up his hand, but because she, sorry I mean he, is so sweet and cuddly he never gets into trouble.

'Shhh, Alaric. Don't tell your word!' Our teacher put a finger to her lip. 'Now, children,' she went on, 'when you have found your word, what I want you to do is to write a story about it!'

Well, there were definitely no gasps of delight, but great gasps of INDIGNATION! What a thing to do!

Trick us all into thinking we were going to play a game and now she expected us to write something! Ethelred went straight back to sleep in protest and I don't blame him, but I am not like that. I face trouble as it comes.

Of course, Leo and Cinnamon IMMEDIATELY started writing, they just can't help themselves, and they write so loudly you can hear their pens scratching.

Anupam wrote in beautiful swirly writing with her green apple-scented pen: 'DAPPLED' on the top of the page and clearly felt that was effort enough because then she returned to the bag of meringues she keeps under her desk. She eats them very slowly, letting them dissolve in her mouth before she swallows, and she can make one packet last for days. I don't know why she doesn't have terrible holes in her teeth. Alaric says she will develop a Behavioural Disorder eating all that refined sugar but it must be a very slow-developing disorder because she's the most well-behaved person I've ever seen. Her name means 'Beyond Compare' in Sanskrit, which is a sacred tongue, she told me. I would like to learn a sacred tongue, but I don't suppose I'll have the time.

Alaric said, 'I REALLY can't find a word!' as if he was about to burst into tears so of course our teacher went over and sat down next to him and helped him for the next twenty minutes.

I kept on turning the pages, but I found it difficult to concentrate, because of Leo's scratchy pen, so I poked him in the back. 'Can you slow down a bit?' I complained, 'You're giving me a headache!' But he didn't even turn around; he only looked up briefly from time to time to see how many pages Cinnamon had written, like the way you look up when you're in a swimming race to see if you're beating anyone, although the pool's always empty by the time I get to the finishing line and they've already started the next race.

I decided not to delay any further, but leave it in the Lap of the Gods, which sounds a perfectly pleasant place to be. I picked up a pen and I flipped the pages of the dictionary to and fro so they made a little breeze and I closed my eyes and stabbed downwards – Bang!

I opened my eyes. The pen had landed between two words – 'cadastre' and 'cactus'. I couldn't really understand what 'cadastre' was except that it was something to do with taxation, and I wasn't going to write a story about that, was I? So I chose 'cactus'. I began to write, and this is what I wrote:

chapter four

. . . MY STORY (AND SOME OTHERS) . . .

'CALX THE CACTUS'

Calx was a cactus who lived in a desert all by himself except for assorted scorpions who weren't very good at conversation. To pass the time, he used to sing hymns as someone had left a hymn book conveniently close by. He only knew one tune so he sang them all to it. He had one favourite, and that was 'Loving Shepherd of Thy Sheep' and he used to sing it twelve times when he woke up and thirty-seven times when he went to bed.

Occasionally he would give concerts and all the scorpions would come and listen. As they weren't very musical, it didn't matter that the hymns were all the same tune, and anyway, they weren't very good at conversation, so they were glad just to have something to listen to.

One day, some ballerinas were travelling through the desert and heard Calx singing. One, whose name was Hlejkipachupihk, said to the other, whose name wasn't Hlejkipachupihk, 'Did you hear that cactus? It's got the best altosoprano metatzobass falsetto tone I've ever heard.' And they made him sign a contract to an opera company.

So Calx's humble name was spread far and wide and millions of people came to hear him. For company, he was given an avocado pear tree (which was slightly better at conversation than the scorpions).

One night, when Calx played the major role in 'Rigoletto', he sang as he had never sung before, and as a reward, the rest of the cast presented him with another cactus to talk to. This was the first cactus Calx had ever seen, and quite suddenly, he was overcome with an irresistible urge to eat it!

And then, in front of an audience of 40,000, Calx the cactus performed the most horrible act of cannibalism ever recorded.

Unfortunately, he was allergic to cactuses, and he turned pink, then blue then orange and dropped dead. Immediately all his prickles shot off him, stabbing over 22,000 people, killing 10,102.

Calx was duly cremated and at the funeral the bagpipe played out melodic strains of 'Loving Shepherd of Thy Sheep' and one of the scorpions who had attended the mass funeral said to the avocado pear tree next to him: 'I think I've heard that somewhere before.'

THE END.

Well! I put down my pen with a clatter. I had never written anything so long! Or so quickly.

'Have you finished, Claudie?' asked our teacher, beaming at me. 'Perhaps you'd like to read it out loud to the class?'

I shook my head, quickly. I'm not the reading aloud type. Anyway, I'd only just finished it – it was long and quick, but what if it was terrible?

Unfortunately, this thought clearly did not occur to several other people in the class, although perhaps it should have. We had to sit and listen to theirs and I'm afraid to say some of the tales showed a person's darker side.

Cinnamon's, for example, was based on the word 'google' and was all about an explorer who was in a race with another explorer to reach the North Pole, but they arrived at the same time, and instead of shaking hands one of them pushed the other one into a hole in the ice and went back to Civilisation, a happy and successful celebrity. In case you're wondering what that had to do with 'google', 'google' was the word the explorer who got pushed in cried out just before he went under the freezing ice, which is Eskimo language for 'I loved and trusted you, I did my best for you, and this is how you reward me!' Well, I don't know how Cinnamon ever learnt Eskimo language, although I wouldn't mind learning it myself; after Sanskrit, that is.

Leo's story was about the word 'Shibboleth' and was the adventures of a diptheria germ who went around the world infecting people, shouting 'HAha! HAha! HAha! Shibboleth!' There wasn't much more to it than that – I suppose that's how he managed to write so many pages – but everybody laughed a lot when he read it, in his special coffee radio advertisement voice, particularly the 'HAha' bits which were positively spine-tingling. Well, not my spine, I thought it was very immature, but that's what our teacher said when she was trying to find something nice to say, because she likes to be encouraging.

Then Alaric read his – it was called: 'Hacienda'.

'Once upon a time there was a princess called Hacienda who went into everybody's house and opened up the cupboards and smashed all the plates, one by one. Then she smashed the glasses, one by one. Then she smashed the cups, one by one. Then she smashed ...'

But our teacher interrupted, which is not polite, and said, 'Alaric, dear, that will do for now. Could you just give me that?' and we all knew that was one piece of literature on its way to the psychologist.

Boaz didn't pick a word; he just wrote another story about rubber bands. That's all he ever writes about. Ethelred said he lost his and we all know what that means, and Abigail said hers was too sad to read, it was all about a dying Sunday School teacher, and if she read it she might break down, so our teacher said, 'That's fine Abigail, just give it to me to read', but then Abigail did break down and the teacher forgot all about it.

Then our teacher said: 'Well, Anupam, what about yours?' And Anupam said very quickly, 'Why don't we turn one of the stories into a play?' because she likes a spectacle. Our teacher, who thinks it's good to be democratic, (although if you ask me, some people in our class aren't ready for democracy), said, 'Well, let's have a vote!'

So we all voted for Boaz's story about the rubber bands because there were so many characters and our teacher looked like she was beginning to agree with me about democracy. Then she turned to me and frowned, and I really didn't want to read my story, I really didn't at all. But she had that look – I'm sure you know the kind of look I mean – so I was just beginning to drag myself up on my feet to start to read when –

Something happened.

chapter five

... I HAVE A STRANGE ENCOUNTER WITH A
MAD WOMAN ...

The thing that happened was an announcement over the
loudspeaker.

In our school we never see our Principal, we just have
announcements. In every classroom, there's a loudspeaker,
and our principal talks into a microphone and out comes
his voice. It only happens when there is a disaster, like
the weather is so hot that we all have to go home, or
the canteen has run out of cheese sandwiches so could
people please change their order.

Or if someone has been bad, really very bad, the
principal says, 'Could X please come to my office
immediately.' (X meaning the extremely bad, really bad
person.) It's very exciting when this happens, and we all
crane our necks to see out the windows to catch a glimpse
of the truly terribly bad person going to the Principal's

office. Although because I am nice, I try not to do this.

Anyway, the loudspeaker crackled and whistled and we all looked up at it because our teacher says you must always look at someone when they are speaking to you even if it's a box and it said 'Could ... er ...'

Silence. Could ... er? What had happened?

'Perhaps he died,' said Boaz, and remember, his father is a comedian.

'Shhhh!' Our teacher raised her finger to her lips.

The loudspeaker crackled again. 'Could ... er ... the ... er ... child who had her photo in the local paper this morning ...'

I gasped. Everyone (the ones who were awake – about half a dozen, by now) turned and stared at me.

'Could ... er ... she come and see me now, please.'

'Claudie!' cried our teacher, DEVASTATED. No one in her class had ever been called to the Principal's office before, I suppose. Well, evil is not that fully developed in kindergarten.

My legs were prickly and my tongue was wobbling. But I stood up and held my head steady.

'Can I go with her?' asked Anupam. As I said, Anupam is fond of a spectacle.

'I don't think so,' said our teacher, shaking her head sadly. 'Claudie must face this alone.'

'Indeed, I must,' I replied firmly. 'Do not fear! Truth shall prevail. It shall not fail me!'

Well, I didn't actually say that, but when you're telling a story I think it's all right to put in a few extra

29

bits. I couldn't say anything – I was terrified. I knew I hadn't done anything bad, but in situations like this you feel guilty anyway. In fact, I started feeling bad because I hadn't done anything bad.

I tottered out of the classroom on my weak little legs, everyone staring at me, wondering what my punishment would be. I might have to spend every lunchtime for two weeks picking up rubbish from the playground. If that happened, I would insist on wearing protective clothing. Or I might have to go to the library and research my ancestors and give a talk at assembly. Or I might . . . I kept walking with my trembling stomach right up to the Principal's office, conveniently located next to the school canteen. It has a brown door with the one dreadful word – OFFICE – written on it.

Although we had never seen him, we knew the Principal was in there, because every day we saw the canteen mothers taking in his lunch. I think he should come out and get it himself and so do the mothers – we know because Abigail's mother told Abigail he just liked being waited on by ladies and if he thought she was going to make him cups of tea every day he had another think coming. Abigail tells us everything her mother says, which is handy.

I stood in front of the brown door in a daze. What would happen to me in there? Someone who lurks all day behind a brown door and doesn't even come out to eat and only communicates through a loudspeaker, well, there has to be something wrong with him, doesn't there?

Perhaps he had some ghastly disfigurement, like in Beauty and the Beast. Maybe if I smiled and tilted my head on one side like an alluring princess it might calm him down.

So I tilted my head and smiled, and I knocked. Just three little taps, hoping that he might not hear them and I could go back to our teacher and say that the Principal wasn't there. But I suppose principals are used to these sorts of tactics and have highly developed hearing as a result, because, 'Come in!' came a deep voice, rather clearer than it was over the familiar loudspeaker.

I pushed the door open. If only I could faint, like Alaric does – now that would make him feel sorry for me! But I can't, so I stepped in and I looked our Principal straight in the eye. Well, through his black sunglasses. Why does he wear sunglasses inside? I wondered, but, 'Yes, yes, come in, come in.' He waved a hand impatiently from behind his huge desk. He did not appear to be horribly disfigured, but I'm no expert. I prefer to look into people's souls.

'Now, what's your name?' Well, I was APPALLED. There he was, ready to heap a cruel punishment upon me and he didn't even know my name!

'Claudie,' I said meekly, not tilting my head any more and reverting to my natural gloomy expression.

'Claudie,' he repeated. 'Look up, for heaven's sake, Claudie!'

I looked up, although the pattern on the linoleum floor was actually very interesting. I looked up and I saw that our Principal and I were not alone in the room.

'Hallo, there!' said a mysterious stranger.

I always like the parts with the mysterious strangers in the movies. You know, the elegant women in veils and big hats who turn up at the wedding and pull out a gun or a vial of poison. This woman wasn't exactly like that – no hat, no veil – just ordinary in ordinary clothes, greenish lipstick and a hideous blue handbag (that might have had a knife in it).

'Claudie!' said the mysterious stranger, coming towards me alarmingly fast. She held in her hand a copy of that morning's local paper. 'As soon as I saw the picture in the paper I knew it had to be!'

I felt myself becoming pale. She knew it Had To Be. How awful that sounded – like the voice at the Crack of Doom. What could it mean? Was I adopted and my parents had never told me? This was my real mother? I wondered where she lived, and if she had a swimming pool. Would I have to share a room? Was she a vegetarian?

'Is your father's name Norbert?' asked the mysterious visitor surprisingly, interrupting my very-fast-train of thought.

Well! what a personal question! Now it just so happens my father's name is Norbert, but I was not about to tell her that, so I said, 'No it's not, it's Oswald.'

She stopped. Her mouth opened. 'But,' she said, 'it must be! It must surely be!'

She turned back to our Principal who was eating a cheese sandwich – perhaps he is the kind of man who turns unconsciously to food in times of stress. Or perhaps he is just very rude.

'It must be Norbert's child! She must be! There couldn't be two people in the world who look like that!'

Now that wasn't very complimentary, and if you saw my father you'd know what I mean.

'She's the IMAGE of him!' the lady went on, staring at me accusingly. 'The absolute IMAGE! She even has the same eye defect!'

'Well, his name's Oswald,' I repeated. I believe it is recommended that once you start to tell a lie, you should stick with it. Eye defect!

'Oswald!' She sniffed. 'Whoever heard of anyone called Oswald!'

'Norbert's an unusual name,' put in the Principal unhelpfully, but I think he just wanted to get her out of the room so he could get on with his duties, ha ha.

'You must have records!' cried the lady, who was clearly not going to give in easily. She waved the newspaper in the air. 'Look it up! It must be Norbert!'

I had to admit, she was persistent. But I am also persistent. I was going to persist longer than she was. Even if the Principal found twenty pieces of paper that said my father's name was Norbert, I was never going to agree to it. But that didn't happen.

'Oh, I couldn't do that,' said the Principal with a little cough. 'Privacy regulations, you know.'

Privacy regulations! How exciting! It made our Principal sound like he was the head of the Secret Police.

'Privacy regulations!'

The only-slightly-mysterious stranger looked at him with very hard eyes, tightening her grip on her handbag. For a moment, I actually thought she was going to swing it in the air and bash him on the head with it and he would die in a pool of blood and I would be a witness so she would have to bash me on the head too.

But I wouldn't die because I am very persistent, I would just go into a coma for a little while but then I would rise out of my deathbed and identify the murderess in a line-up and my picture would be in the paper again, maybe twice, and I would have more publicity clippings than Abigail.

However, she didn't bash him on the head – she just hissed: 'SSSSSSSsssssssssssssssss' which was really very peculiar. She looked actually rather STRICKEN, if you know what I mean. She turned to me, shaking her head sadly, as if to say, 'I know you're lying!' and then she looked at the Principal again not so much sadly as VICIOUSLY and muttered, 'Obstructive!'

He adjusted his sunglasses and nodded as if she had just said, 'Thank you so much for all your assistance'. I suppose he nodded because in our school Co-operation is one of our Core Values. Co-operation means agreeing with somebody when you can't be bothered to persist.

The lady didn't give him a second glance. She heaved her handbag up onto her massive shoulder and made a hummphing kind of noise and marched briskly out of the Office, slamming the door behind her.

I stayed where I was. Not that I wanted to be with

our Principal, but because I didn't want that woman to seize on me in the playground and start to torture me for the truth – who knows what she kept in that handbag for terrorising children? But our Principal snapped and waved his half-eaten cheese sandwich at me.

'Off you go, then! Don't muck around! Back to class!'

Clearly he had completely lost interest in the whole episode. What could I do? At least I wasn't getting any punishment. So before he could change his mind, I turned and stumbled outside.

I didn't go straight back to class, though. I ran over to a large leafy tree and hid behind it and peered around. The mysterious stranger, as I suspected, had not yet left the school. She was standing at the gates, gazing BALEFULLY back in the direction of the office. Well, I couldn't exactly see from that distance if her gaze was baleful, but you can guess those sorts of things.

She stood there like a lion on a hill as though she was thinking hard, planning something, something dreadful. I stayed right behind that tree, feeling sick. Why didn't she leave?

Then suddenly, as though she'd made up her mind, she swung her handbag and turned and stalked out the gates to the car park. She got into a yellow car, a rather shiny silly-looking car that could have been designed by the makers of Lego. She turned on the engine and let it growl for a while, and I was quaking and thinking, Go! Go! Go! and at last she did, she reversed back onto the street and drove away in a cloud of smoke and dust.

chapter six

Now, I expected that back in my classroom, everyone would be waiting in awed silence, wondering what I had done and what was going to happen to me. However, as I said before, half of my class is usually asleep and wouldn't know if we'd been invaded by Visigoths, (which are a kind of invading tribe, in case you didn't know) and the other half I suppose are just too interested in their own concerns to care whether I was alive or dead. There aren't that many caring people in the world, I've noticed, and I can tell you it's a heavy burden being one of the sensitive ones.

I came in the door to find our teacher calmly writing on the blackboard. She'd obviously given up on the dictionary game and decided to do sums instead as a simpler exercise – I could have told her that. Anyway, when she realised I'd come back alive, she turned and raised her eyebrows at me, which was her way, I suppose, of saying 'Well, what happened?' and a few people looked up and I said dramatically, 'A case of mistaken identity!'

Well, I thought it was dramatic but nobody paid much attention. They were all writing down things from the board: scribble, scribble. I sat down at my desk next to Anupam and got out my maths book and borrowed one of Anupam's special pens – she has hundreds of special pens so I don't suppose they're that special, really. She's got absolutely every colour you could think of. It's what she spends all her pocket money on and I think it's what you call a fetish. I picked up one of her pens and sat there chewing on the end of it, forgetting that Anupam had forbidden me to do that but I was tense after my encounter.

Now I wonder, I thought – I didn't say it, because if you talk out loud to nobody, people think you are mad, although they should just mind their own business. Anyway, I thought, I wonder if I should tell my father about this?

Should I tell him? Who was this person in the yellow Lego car? She seemed to know his name, but would he want to know hers? I remembered her hair and her handbag, her greenish lips and her generally accusing manner. I had a feeling about that woman. There was something about her that made me pretty sure that she had come out of that terrible place, The Past.

My father has a dreadful Past. He is not at all nostalgic, which is a word for people who find themselves humming

37

along with the song 'Those Were The Days, My Friend!' when it's on the radio. With him it's quite the opposite. Sometimes we've had to leave restaurants very quickly when he thought he saw someone from The Past. Once we left so quickly I didn't even get to eat my chips, which I had been specially saving for the end. He just leapt out of the chair and said, in the middle of a mouthful, 'We're getting out of here!' and dashed for the door using me as a Human Shield.

I had my suspicions, you see, about this Lego Lady and why she wanted to know if my father's name was Norbert. As I said before, in business, sometimes people aren't so happy with how things turn out. I don't know why exactly, but I know it's to do with money. Now my father is a philosophical person, as you know, and his attitude is 'It's all for the Best' but others in this world are not so philosophical. They think it's not all for the best, and they sometimes harbour thoughts of VENGEANCE. My father says people like that are not modern. I had the feeling that the Lego Lady might not be very modern at all.

And just now was one of those times when my father would be particularly anxious not to run into anybody difficult – imagine all the deep-breathing on the balcony it would take to calm him down if I told him that a strange woman with a navy handbag was on his trail! Not to mention he would blame it all on me for having my picture in the paper ...

I groaned. I sucked on Anupam's pen. I couldn't tell

him. I would have to keep it to myself. It happens that way in life, that the stronger parties, like me, have to take charge of the weaker parties, like my father. It was my burden. The word 'burden' cheered me up a little – it made me sound so saintly all of a sudden, shouldering another's 'burden'.

In the middle of all these mixed-up thoughts, I suddenly swallowed a glob of lilac ink, which was VERY unpleasant and for the moment stopped me thinking altogether. I had to run out to the taps and wash my mouth out and it was so VILE. Then I had to put my head down on my desk and have a little rest from my sums and everything, actually. That's about all I remember from that day.

Until, that is, the bell rang for the end of school. Despite my resting, I was EXHAUSTED, just like Griselda, who I always have to wait for at the gate to walk her home because she never looks where she's going. If it wasn't for me, she'd be squashed a hundred times over by now.

Griselda was bringing a friend home. She only ever brings home the same friend, a girl her age called Winsome. Winsome is the sister of Ethelred, the sleepy person who slumps at the back of our classroom. Winsome and Ethelred share the same musty sort of smell, as though they spend most of their time crawling under the house with a torch looking for stick insects.

'CLAUDIE!!!!!!!'

Griselda leapt on top of me near the gate as if I was

trying to leave without her and maybe I was.

'Yes, yes, all right,' I said crossly. 'Come on, you two.'

We dawdled out of the school grounds. Griselda doesn't mind Winsome's mustiness, she is too young, but I kept my distance. I didn't want to have to listen to their childish chatter. Although all the chatter actually came out of Griselda's mouth, as Winsome never says anything – I suppose that's why Griselda likes her.

'CLAUDIE!!!!!!!!!!!!'

I jumped. Griselda and musty little Winsome were now standing on the edge of the road waiting for me like a pair of tadpoles to take them safely over.

'You don't have to shout,' I said in low gentlewomanly tones that drive Griselda mad, and I grabbed hold of her hand and she grabbed hold of Winsome's.

The cars sped by, all in a great hurry to get somewhere or other, probably the next Engaged Buddhist meeting, as there is a monastery quite near by. I was just thinking that Engaged Buddhists shouldn't be in a hurry to get anywhere at all but should be leaning out the window taking deep breaths when a car slowed right down next to us and hooted and all three of us half-fell back on to the footpath.

It was the yellow Lego car! With that dreadful woman inside it! And she was beckoning at me in a positively threatening way.

'Come over here!' she called out in a cackle and we stared, shocked. Anyone would be, not just someone with something to hide.

'Claudie, I think that lady wants to talk to you,' Griselda pointed out but, 'Run!' I screamed and I yanked her and she yanked Winsome and we all began to run.

'What are you doing, Claudie!' panted Griselda. 'That lady just wants to ask you something.'

I shouted something rude to Griselda which I can only hope Winsome forgets to tell her mother about, assuming she can actually talk. It was effective, anyway and that's the main thing in an emergency, because they both came running after me at a great pace, our bags bouncing up and down on our backs.

chapter seven

. . . INTO A DARK AND UNPLEASANT
PLACE . . .

You may think, surely the lady in the yellow Lego car
could simply have driven to catch up with us, but I had
craftily chosen a one-way street to run down – a one-
way street going the wrong way, if you know what I
mean. We ran and ran until we reached the corner where
there was a general store that I had seen many times
but never been inside because it looked so dirty and
tattered and the pictures of the ice-creams looked about
thirty years old, I thought it must be deceased but no!
The door was open and in we bolted.

How dark it was in that shop! I thought perhaps it
was deceased after all, but there was someone sitting on
a stool behind a counter covered with jars of rotting figs
and dried bananas. This person did not look very friendly
and no wonder he never got any customers because he

just barked out, 'What do you want?' which is no way to conduct a retail business if you ask me. What about 'Can I help you?' or, 'What a lovely day!'

'I want some peanuts. I'm starving to death,' mentioned Griselda, because of course she'd managed to find an ancient bag of peanuts in the darkest corner of the darkest shop in the world.

'Shhhhhh, I don't have any money!' I retorted. 'Just stay still, can't you?' and I shuffled them into the corner.

'What do you want?' repeated the man, I'm pretty sure it was a man but with those clothes how can you tell?

I replied as coldly as I could, 'We're thinking about it,' which is a useful phrase – you should keep it in mind. The person got off the stool and shuffled over to where Winsome had sat herself down upon some packets of spaghetti and was making crunching sounds.

'Get up from there!' growled the person and Winsome had that about-to-burst-into-tears face.

I could have said a few things, like 'You shouldn't keep spaghetti on the floor where anyone might sit on it, you should keep cans of pet food.' But rather than get drawn into that kind of conversation (I've noticed people never react well to having their faults pointed out), I decided that the danger, meaning the Lego lady, should surely have passed by then and we could leave. So I pulled Griselda and she pulled Winsome and we all got out of the corner and banged past the Weird Shopkeeper into the sunshine again.

I had a quick and careful look for the yellow car but

it was nowhere. There were no cars at all in this dreary little one-way street with its horrible shop on the corner. I could imagine the Lego Lady cursing to herself, crying out 'Foiled again!' like they do on cartoons.

'We'll go the back way home,' I said to the little ones and Griselda said, 'I didn't know there was a back way,' and actually there isn't, only it took quite a long time to find that out and Griselda whined and moaned the whole time and I would have hit her except for Winsome being a witness.

When we did finally get home, Winsome's mother was already there to pick her up, standing at the bottom of our block of flats next to my mother and neither of them looked pleased to see us.

Winsome's mother, who is very small and has a very high voice, squeaked, 'Where have you been! I've been so worried!'

I said to my mother, 'I took them to the park to play.'

Then I managed somehow accidentally to step on Griselda's toes very very hard which started her screaming and Winsome's mother snatched Winsome away and off they went. I think Winsome's mother is someone who thinks that people who live in blocks of flats are somehow not to be trusted, but even Griselda would never sit on a packet of spaghetti. Anyway, our mother sighed and shook her head and said something under her breath and I can't lip read, can I? so I didn't answer. Then Griselda and I (kicking each other) followed our mother up the stairs inside.

My father was in the living room watching the television and beating a rug. I don't think you are supposed to beat a rug inside because all the dust flies into your face which can't be healthy, but the neighbours complain when he beats it on the balcony. We are on the middle floor, you see. If you are on the middle floor, you have to be careful about what you do on the balcony, but deep breathing is all right.

'Hallo-there-where-have-you-been?' our father asked us – that's how he talks and Griselda is so stupid I knew she was about to say something about the Lego Lady so before she could get very far I leaned over her until she toppled on the floor and I lay right on top of her and I said in her ear in my softest, most sinister voice, 'Don't say ANYTHING about the woman in the car. ANYTHING!' and I pinched her arms with my fingernails just to make sure. Griselda is quite compliant in situations like this, I knew I could trust her now. At least I didn't have to worry about Winsome, because she never opens her mouth.

I went to my room and sat down on the bed for a moment, trying to still my beating heart. I think that might be a quote from someone like Shakespeare, who served literature and never became a Baron. Then I went over to the window and looked out. Had the Lego Lady found us? Had she somehow followed us and now lurked out there as the sun was setting, waiting to descend upon my happy home? There was no sign of her on the street now. But tomorrow at school, would she be there again?

I chewed my nails, and gazed at the newspaper photograph I had stuck on the wardrobe. If only I didn't look like him so much! Because it was true what the Lego Lady had said – we had the same everything, my father and I, not just an eye defect – same eyebrows, nose, mouth, chin. All I had of my mother were my long skinny toes . . .

What was I going to do? I couldn't tell my mother, she would just tell my father because that's the way parents are. I couldn't tell anyone. But how many times would I be able to escape her? Sooner or later the Lego Lady would get me, or at any rate, follow me home and find my father and DISASTER.

Now our teacher says life is a series of challenges, although admittedly she is talking about long division, on the whole. Still, this was a challenge and I would have to solve it, I told myself desperately, one way or the other. I had to get rid of this troublesome Lego Lady. Perhaps an idea would come to me in my sleep, if I banged my head on the pillow five times just after turning out the light. Maybe if I banged my head ten times . . .

'CLAUDIE! CLAUDIE!'

I grimaced. I was going to have to think up some sort of explanation for Griselda. I went over and opened the door and she squeezed her way in and ran over and jumped up on my bed.

'Who was that lady?' she asked outright, because Griselda is not subtle, not subtle at all.

'She's a maniac,' I replied calmly. 'She goes around kidnapping children and if you go near her or tell Mum and Dad you've seen her, I'll ... I'll ...'

'What?' asked Griselda, bouncing up and down in her mindless way and not looking especially upset at the thought of being kidnapped by a maniac.

'I'll spit on your toothbrush,' I said, and that worked, of course, because Griselda is an oral person and funny about germs. She turned white and made a strange internal sound.

'Girls! Dinner!' called out my mother from the kitchen over the top of the soap opera on the television. My father likes to watch soap operas because he is so passionate.

'I'm warning you!' I said to Griselda as we left our room for our baked beans which is our favourite dinner, and I believe, SUPREMELY nutritious, which means good for you.

'I promise!' said Griselda, and she is an honest girl, although only because she is so young and I'm afraid, not very intelligent. When you are old and clever, being honest is much more difficult.

chapter eight

. . . HOWEVER, LIFE GOES ON . . .

The next morning, I woke up without a single idea. I knew it wouldn't work. After all, Alaric is always banging his head and getting concussion – and I don't remember one good idea he's ever had afterwards.

My mother had already taken Griselda to school early to play softball or some other awful game that she likes, so it was just my father and me and the television while we ate our cereal. Usually, this is a good and peaceful way to start the day, not that in my father's case there was much of a day to start, just sitting around hiding. I glanced at him sideways, with a mixture of pity and irritation. How did he get himself into these tangles? Why wasn't he rolling in money? Then he could just pay all his enemies off, including the Lego Lady, and happily go and make some new ones.

I arrived late at school, as somehow it's hard to get

out the front door when the television's on. The bell had already gone so I ambled with APLOMB into the classroom (if I hurried, then our teacher would notice I was late) and sat down as usual next to Anupam.

The teacher was asking everybody what their ambition was – she does this from time to time. Anupam had just put up her hand and was saying, 'My ambition is to swim one length of an Olympic pool.'

Now I know perfectly well Anupan can already swim one length of an Olympic pool, even two, but she likes to get in early so that our teacher leaves her alone and she can relax and eat meringues.

'Very good, Anupam,' our teacher smiled. 'Does anyone else have an ambition?'

Alaric said, 'My ambition is to split the atom.'

Alaric didn't know what that meant, neither did we and neither did our teacher, but she nodded intelligently just in case someone did.

Then Leo said, 'I'm going to be the greatest priest in the world,' which I think is a rather worldly sort of ambition, don't you? But then Cinnamon said, 'My ambition is to own seven Rolls Royce limousines,' which made Leo's ambition look positively spiritual.

'Boaz?' said our teacher, because she likes to encourage the quiet ones, more fool her.

Boaz muttered, as usual, and we all knew it would have something to do with his rubber band collection. What else? And maybe even our teacher guessed, because she didn't ask him to speak up. I suppose she didn't want to be shouted at, like the reporter had been.

Abigail put up her hand. She had clearly been thinking hard, so that her ambition would be better than anyone else's.

'I'm going to discover a cure for polio,' she said, and Anupam said, between mouthfuls of green meringue, 'They've already discovered that about fifty years ago,' and poor Abigail was CRESTFALLEN and Alaric said, 'How about a cure for hiccups?' and Abigail WITHERED him with a look because let's face it, hiccups is not exactly polio.

'One man had hiccups for twenty-two years,' said Alaric. 'I read it in the Guinness Book of Records.'

'When I get hiccups my dad makes me drink a glass of milk backwards,' said Cinnamon.

'When I get hiccups I have to leave the room,' said Leo, which I can understand, because hiccups in Leo usually leads to something worse.

'How do you drink a glass of milk backwards?' asked Alaric, who is very curious and just won't let things be.

Most days in our classroom are like this, I'm afraid. Luckily nobody asked me about my ambition, which, as you know, is to become a Baroness. But my ambition is a secret, because I'm afraid of Losing Face, which is what they fear in Japan, according to Alaric's psychologist, although they should be more frightened of Godzilla if you ask me. Anyway, it's good to have a secret ambition – everyone should have one. I saw a lady on television once who said her secret ambition was to throw an egg in an electric fan.

By the time the bell went in the afternoon, I had it all planned. I ran as fast as I could out of the room and grabbed hold of Griselda under the fig tree. 'Come this way!' I told her, tugging at her by her bag. If only our mother would let me use a lead like a dog, but she just won't.

'Why?' Griselda began to whine but I didn't listen. I pulled her along into the music room, which is normally locked but I knew it wouldn't be that day because there was a practice of the recorder band and they need all the practice they can get.

I dragged Griselda up the steps and into the music room. The teacher who has to take them, Mr Tolty, looked at us and said what did we want.

'Can we just stay and listen for a bit?' I asked nicely, because that was my plan, you see, to lurk in the music room until all the children had gone and the Lego Lady waiting in her car outside would give up and go home herself.

'Why?' said Mr Tolty, as if he couldn't believe that anyone would want to do such a thing.

'Griselda's thinking of learning the recorder,' I said. 'I thought it might be good if she had a little listen first.'

Anyone looking at Griselda can tell she's completely unmusical and I must say Mr Tolty shuddered, I suppose imagining the ghastly sight of Griselda with a recorder in her mouth but he said, 'Yes, yes, all right.' Then he banged on the music stand in front of him as all the other children came hurtling in and the practice began.

Well, I think the less I dwell on those particular twenty minutes the better. I don't think any good comes out of remembering painful experiences, whatever Alaric's psychologist says. Let's just say they played 'The Happy Wanderer' and 'Food Glorious Food' and leave it at that. Griselda loved it, of course, I told you she was mad, she thought it was just sooo beautiful.

'When can I join?' she tried to ask Mr Tolty but luckily it was too noisy as everyone ran out the door for him to hear, and I dragged her away again outside.

'When can I join?' she asked me. 'I want to play the recorder.'

'Shhhhhh!' I put a hand over her mouth. 'I'm looking for the maniac!'

Keeping Griselda behind me, I crept out from behind the music room and had a quick look around the playground which, apart from the members of the recorder band, was now deserted. No sign of the Lego Lady, and no sign of the Lego car in the car-park either, to my great relief. No cars at all, actually, because the teachers at our school are as desperate to get away in the afternoons as the children, poor things. I'd foiled her again!

'Okay, we can go,' I ordered Griselda. 'She's not there.'

'When can I join, I want to play the recorder!' said Griselda, and when she said it about seven more times and she finally realised I wasn't going to answer she said, 'When is the lady going to stop wanting to kidnap us?'

'I don't know,' I said, 'but it won't go on forever.'

I hoped. So far it had only been two afternoons, and it was draining the life out of me. I'm not used to that level of excitement.

chapter nine

. . . I LOOK OUT THE PEEPHOLE . . .

Well, I have to hurry the story along a bit now, because nothing happened for the next two days, which were Friday and Saturday. At least, things happened but you can't include everything in literature, you have to make choices for artistic reasons. So I'm making a few choices, and not just for artistic reasons. I'm leaving out the bits when Leo had a stomach upset, Alaric got concussion (again), Cinnamon got a special mention in assembly for being so wonderful at everything (who cares!) and my mother bought Griselda a recorder. I suppose there must have been some happy times too, but I can't remember any.

On Friday it was sport. I knew the Lego Lady would be lurking. So when the bell rang and the playground was crowded with hot exhausted bodies and shouting and hats and cars everywhere, including you-know-who's, I swiftly covered Griselda's head with a jumper so she looked like the ghost of a blue midget. Then I covered my own head with a jumper too so I looked like the ghost of a slightly taller blue midget, and we escaped unnoticed in the general confusion like Roman soldiers outwitting someone whose name I can't remember just at this moment in the battlefields of Gaul.

But my nerves were wearing down. At least now it was the weekend, so I had some time to think of what I was going to do about the situation, because I couldn't go on like this. The weekend I knew would be quiet and good for thinking, because my mother would be taking Griselda out with her to work.

My mother doesn't normally work on weekends, but because my father was in hiding, my mother was back in the seed business. Remember I told you how she likes seeds? Well, when we're running out of money, she sells them. She sells them on the bus, so she doesn't need to spend money on renting a shop or even advertisements. All she has to spend is the bus fare, and she gets a discounted ticket because my father is unemployed.

It is her own business invention. This is how it works: she gets on the bus (any bus, it doesn't matter where it's going) and she sits in the second seat from the front (this is the best seat for her business, she's tried them all – she's a very scientific woman). Anyway, she waits until someone comes and sits next to her, and you know how it is on buses, if you're not too peculiar people start chatting, and my mother has that nice chatty sort of look about her. Actually she looks just like a normal person.

So she gets talking and pretty soon the conversation gets around to seeds and flowers (or vegetables – she's versatile) and then she whips out a packet of seeds from her coat pocket (they are very light so she can carry lots and lots) and even a catalogue and before you know it, she's taking orders! Sometimes. Well, if you're enthusiastic, you can sell anything, that's what they say, at least that's what my father says. I suppose enthusiastic is another word for passionate, and she's certainly passionate about seeds.

My mother doesn't go on trains selling seeds because she says they're too noisy for intimate conversations, although I don't know what's so intimate about pansies and runner beans. Perhaps people tell her all their secrets – if so, she shouldn't listen because someone might tell her something TERRIBLE, like, 'I poisoned my grandmother last night,' and my mother would say, 'Oh, how interesting. Can I show you a selection of baby beets?'

She takes Griselda with her because although Griselda doesn't actually sell anything, she is apparently charming and people love a charming child. I actually think people, without exception, LOATHE a charming child, but you can't tell a mother that. My mother says people warm to Griselda because of her beautiful red hair, though in my opinion it's a BILIOUS shade. (Bilious means it makes you sick in the stomach.)

So on Saturday my mother and Griselda went out to work and my father and I spent the day inside watching television and playing poker, using matchsticks to bet with, and eating plates of cheese and chips. My mother and Griselda came home late, and my mother's face was rather stony, so we knew she hadn't sold much. We had rice pudding with a bit too much cinnamon and not quite enough sugar for dinner.

The next day I'd invited Alaric to come over and play. You might think it's funny that I wanted to invite a boy, but really, if you met Alaric you wouldn't think so. And I felt sorry for him, because it was going to be Father's Day, and his father is in the cemetery and the psychologist told his mother they shouldn't go there any more because it was time to Move On.

Sunday is a good day for Alaric to visit, because in the morning he does flamenco classes in the scout hall just around the corner from where we live, then he can come over when his class had finished. He is doing flamenco classes because he had a test at school and they said he was Uncoordinated, which is a mean thing to say about someone, isn't it? Alaric seems to have a lot of defects – he has to blow ping-pong balls up and down the kitchen table every morning because his lungs are very weak, and he has to wear a wire thing in his mouth at night because otherwise his teeth might grow the wrong way like a rodent – and these are just his physical problems.

Anyway, because it was Father's Day, Griselda got

up early to make our father breakfast in bed, but all she brought him was a banana and she didn't even peel it, so that wasn't such a big effort. I gave him the spider on the stick that we'd made at school out of the old egg-cartons and he tried to look grateful but I suppose he is under a lot of stress. My mother gave him a kiss, a very mothery sort of present.

Then she and Griselda went off on the bus to work. My father was sleepy – he believes in resting on Sundays even if he hasn't done anything in particular during the week. As there are no soap operas on Sundays, he lay on the sofa watching a telecast of a church service in a foreign language. I had nothing to do but wait for Alaric, so I squeezed up on the sofa next to him and began to feel rather sleepy myself – funny how churches, even on the television, can do that to a person.

My eyes were sliding closed and my breathing was slowing down, and the voices were beginning to blur, when the doorbell rang.

BRRRRRRRRR!

Naturally I thought it must be Alaric, even though it was too early and I hadn't heard the clack clack clack of his shiny black shoes on the concrete stairs – he has to wear special shoes for flamenco classes with very thick high heels.

I jumped up off the sofa and ran over to open the door. As I had my fingers on the handle, I had a peek through the peephole because I wanted to see how Alaric looked with his face all fishy.

I peeked through and BOOM! Instead of Alaric's fishy face I found myself peeking at the fishy face of the Lego Lady!

chapter ten

... AND GET MORE THAN I BARGAINED FOR ...

My JAW DROPPED and MY EYES WERE ON STALKS.
I sank soundlessly to the ground. How could this be? How
had she found out where we lived? How, how, how ...

The bell rang again.

BRRRRRRRRRR!

I was shaking on the floor. I looked quickly over at my
father, but he had been sent into the deepest sleep by the
television hymn-singing and was snoring like a baby. In
any case, the church service involved a great deal of tingling
of little bells, signifying the entrance of the Holy Ghost or
something (Leo told me) so even if he heard the doorbell
from his slumber it probably just merged into the general
spiritual atmosphere. Although the Lego Lady was not
exactly anybody's idea of the Holy Ghost.

'Is anyone home?'

That awful, unmistakable voice. That face and that voice. I remembered the green lips, her long white arms. I had to think quickly. I couldn't open the door. She would put her foot in, and then her shoulder and then her handbag, and then there'd be no getting rid of her.

So I stayed absolutely still, sitting on the ground, my back against the door. We have very good locks in our place (my father is fussy about locks), so I knew she wouldn't be able to slide it open with her credit card, or even worse things she might have in her horrible handbag.

'Norbert? Are you there?'

There was a strange rustling sound. What was she doing? Was she getting out a gun? Was she going to shoot him right through the door? What would I say to the police? Would they draw around my father's body with chalk on the floor like they do in movies? Would we have to go and stay with my auntie who only has marmalade for the toast at breakfast and Griselda and I don't like marmalade, not one bit.

'Someone's in there,' I heard her mutter, because of course she could hear the television. She probably thought there was a whole roomful of people down on their knees praying out loud in Cantonese, refusing to open the door, which wouldn't be very Christian of them.

The rustling continued, then a kind of scraping. It was terrible – I clenched my fists. I knew I should move away from the door – but it was as though I was stuck on the spot.

Then a piece of paper came sliding slowly under the

door, right next to where I was sitting. I watched it coming with appalled fascination, like a message coming out of a fax machine. The writing was face up, it was in green texta and big violent print:

NORBERT,
I'M BACK FROM THE HILL COUNTRY! I'LL BE IN TOUCH.
MIMI XXX

Mimi! Mimi?

The Lego Lady's name was Mimi! I almost gulped out loud, but I am nothing if not self-controlled. I didn't even breathe – well, not that I remember. I heard her turning on squeaky shoes, and squelching down the concrete stairs. I still didn't get up. I didn't touch the note. I stayed where I was like a stone, until I heard the sound of the Lego car start up and drive away.

Then I leapt up, into action. This was no time for deep thoughts. I reread the note. 'Hill country?' I didn't like the sound of that at all. And I wasn't taken in for a moment by those green kisses – the kiss of death, that's what they meant. It was worse, far worse than I had thought.

I did the first thing that I knew would work. I ripped the note into pieces, put it in my mouth and chewed it up into a sticky mess and spat it out in the kitchen sink, running the tap over it.

I made sure my father was still fast asleep, then ran over and took the keys from on top of the bookshelf. I padded swiftly out the door, locking all three locks behind me. That way no one could get in, except for me and my mother who had all three keys.

No one could get in, certainly not Mimi even if she came back and banged the door down. Actually no one could get out, either, meaning my father. But that was all right. He shouldn't be going anywhere, anyway.

Then I ran down the stairs, the keys clinking in my pocket. I gasped for air. I ran like a banshee (whatever that is) – down the street, and round the corner to the scout hall. 'Don't look back!' is a practical piece of advice – the ancients invented it, I believe – and I took it.

chapter eleven

. . . I SPEND AN ENTERTAINING AFTERNOON
WITH FRIENDS . . .

I was panting and my chest was aching and when I
reached the scout hall I nearly COLLAPSED but
I composed myself because I didn't want anyone to call
an ambulance. The door was wide open and I crept in,
although I needn't have bothered creeping because the
music was so loud it'd give anyone a headache, even
a deaf person. I'm surprised the neighbours don't complain, but perhaps they don't mind because it drowns
out the noise of the traffic and the aeroplanes and the
barking dogs and the police sirens. You can see that
I live in a stimulating neighbourhood.

Anyway, I sat down on the wooden floor and watched
the class. There was so much banging up and down that
the floorboards vibrated and I lay on my back and felt
like I was having a massage, which was certainly relaxing

after recent traumatic events. Because I was on the floor I could only see people's legs and feet but it was easy to tell which were Alaric's legs (right at the back) because he is very uncoordinated, although I would never say so, not like some people.

I started to calm down, soothed by the banging floor and feelings of pity for Alaric. The flamenco teacher wasn't a very kindly sort of person and did a great deal of unsympathetic shouting. 'FASTER! FASTER! TOGETHER!' Poor Alaric, I was sure his eyes were full of tears and I could feel my own filling up as well, forgetting all about Mimi and Norbert and all the dreadful possibilities. It's useful, I find, to dwell on another person's sorrows when you want to stop dwelling on your own.

'RIGHT! THAT'S IT! CHACHACHA!'

This was the flamenco teacher's way of saying it was all over and she turned off the music, thank heavens, and all the dancers came running towards me CLACK CLACK CLACK CLACK like a merciless herd of wild goats and I leapt up from the floor just in time to save myself from being trampled to death.

'Hi Claudie!' said Alaric.

I did not feel quite so much like cuddling him as usual because he was very sweaty. He did not look broken and humiliated, though, he looked quite happy. I suppose it's possible he enjoys being screamed at by a crazed flamenco teacher.

'Hi,' I said briefly, my heart being so full, although

for a moment I'd forgotten exactly why.

'What are we going to have for lunch?' asked Alaric, who worries a great deal about food – I suppose he needs a lot to maintain his lovely subcutaneous fat.

Then I remembered. The whole terrible scene positively FLASHED into my mind. Mimi! Norbert! Lego Lady XXX – I started panicking.

'What's wrong?' asked Alaric as he pulled out a handkerchief from his pocket to mop his brow, tossing back his lovely hair. Alaric is the only person in our school who has a handkerchief. It is large and square with a red border.

'Well,' I began, and stopped. What was I going to tell Alaric? That I'd locked my father in his own home to save him from assassination? Alaric was delicate – he might not handle the truth very well. Well, who can? Let's face it. So I told him everything and perhaps he's not as delicate as I thought he was because it didn't seem to bother him much and he just said, 'Come to my house instead, then.' He added, 'My mother won't be there. She's gone to look at curtains.'

What a dreary life! Imagine having sunk so low you had to go out looking at curtains for entertainment. I hope I never become a grieving widow.

So off we went. Alaric and his mother live in a teeny-tiny wooden house like a gingerbread cottage about three blocks walk from the scout hall. When we got there Alaric suddenly said, 'I don't have a key!'

What a day of keys I was having!

'There must be an open window somewhere,' I said, because my father, who is not a comedian, always says it's simply amazing how many people go out and lock the front door but leave the windows wide open. Sure enough, we walked around to the back and there was a window not exactly wide open but enough for us and we climbed up and squeezed inside.

Once we were safely there, though, what were we going to do? If you're a teenager, I suppose, you can drink all the Creme de Menthe and take off your clothes and run around naked and cackling, but at our age all we could think of was to watch television and eat chocolate biscuits and once we'd done that, then what were we going to do? I was too tense about you-know-what to play Monopoly or do any colouring-in (these were Alaric's suggestions) so then Alaric said, 'We could visit Abigail,' because Abigail lives in the same street about fifteen doors down.

So we did. We jumped back out of the window because the front door was locked from the inside as well as the outside and wandered down to Abigail's place, which is enormous and fantasically messy and smells of dogs.

Abigail's mother opened the door and said, 'Oh, it's you. She's out the back.' She made a sign with her thumb and disappeared. We went down the dark musty hallway STREWN with bitten-up things and out to the backyard where Abigail was, with her enormous black dog whose name is Odin.

'Hi!' she shouted. 'Odin has had some puppies! Come

and look!' We ran down into the garden which was littered with the huge decaying papier mâché chess pieces and looked a bit like a run-down cemetery which must have made Alaric feel right at home. Abigail was kneeling down in front of the remains of the White Queen.

'Look!' she whispered and we looked and there in the rotting hollow of the White Queen's gown was a nest of six squirming little black puppies, all with their eyes shut and their tiny tails in the air like piglets.

'They were born yesterday,' said Abigail. 'You can have one when they're six weeks old.'

Alaric said, 'My psychologist says I'm not ready for a pet,' and I thought about Mimi XXX and my father and all the tragedy I was going to have to live through in the weeks to come and I decided that probably it wasn't the right time for me to bring a puppy home either.

We played King Arthur and the Knights of the Round Table with great big sticks (Abigail's garden is full of useful objects) and we charged up and down stabbing all the chess pieces and shouting out 'VICTORY!' and 'TAKE THAT, SCOUNDREL!' Abigail's mother brought out some sandwiches and left them on a plate on the concrete just like we were puppies too and we had to get there quickly before Odin gobbled them all down – what a jaw that dog has! And we drank water from the hose and then we sprayed each other and got drenched and Alaric cried and we both cuddled him and we lay in the sun and baked as dry as dry as dry.

Then Alaric said, 'My mother's probably finished looking at curtains now,' which was realistic, because how many curtains can a grieving widow see in one afternoon? So he left, but I stayed, because I didn't want to get home until after my mother and Griselda.

Once Alaric had gone, we were allowed inside. Abigail's mother is scared of boys, because one night some of Abigail's big brother's friends kicked in the television when they got a bit overexcited and Abigail's mother said they have to pay for it to be fixed and that was about three years ago, so all I can say is she's a very optimistic woman.

So we played bowling alleys in the corridor with a couple of soccer balls and tall things like candlesticks and vases until at last Abigail's mother said, 'I'd better run you home, hadn't I, Claudie. It's dinner time!'

And it was – outside it was dark. I looked out the window at the moon. I thought of Mimi. I felt the keys hard and spiky in the bottom of my pocket.

Abigail's mother has a car, which is an asset except that it stinks of DOG and the windows don't have any handles to wind down but maybe she took them off on purpose because otherwise she'd have to give people lifts all the time. She drove me home through the streetlights and the people gathering about on the footpaths. She let me out at our block of flats and said, 'You'll be right now, won't you, Claudie?'

Naturally I wasn't going to tell her anything about Mimi and my family's various EXIGENCIES and I just gulped and said, 'I'm fine!' I gave her a grin so as not to look suspicious and she drove off into the night, and there I was, brave as ever, ready to face the music. I climbed up the steps to our front door. It was open. I closed my eyes and walked in.

chapter twelve

...I TAKE MATTERS INTO MY OWN HANDS...

'What's wrong with Claudie?' asked Griselda as I banged into the wall and opened my eyes.

There they were: my mother, my sister and my perfectly healthy, untouched father, sitting at the table, eating corn on the cob.

'Where did you go?' said my father.

'Alaric's,' I gulped.

'Ah, yes, dear little Alaric,' sighed my father sentimentally, who wouldn't know Alaric from Socrates and there's a bit of a difference, I can tell you.

'I thought Alaric was supposed to come here,' my mother said, not looking very pleased. 'You locked your poor father in! What if there'd been a fire and he couldn't get out? And you should have left a note. I was worried about you.'

'Mum thought you fell off the balcony,' said Griselda.

'I did not,' said my mother. 'That was your idea.'

I put the keys back on the bookshelf and sat down at the table. My father passed me a cob of corn. I stared at it. It looked like rows and rows of yellow teeth.

'Did you sell many seeds today?' I asked my mother, to change the subject.

'Mainly nasturtiums,' said my mother gloomily, because everyone knows nasturtiums are dirt cheap.

Money, I thought to myself later in bed, with wisdom way beyond my years, while Griselda snored the night away. It all comes down to money. If we had money, there'd be no Mimi. Because that was obviously what she wanted – my father had gotten into some sort of pickle and she wanted money.

But how were we ever going to get any money? Not by selling seeds on the bus, that's for sure. How do people make money? Someone rich would know. Now the only person I knew who was rich was Leo.

On Monday morning before school I cornered Leo in the playground. He was sitting as usual by himself on a pile of leaves reading a book. When Leo reads, he hangs onto the book as though it's alive and about to wriggle away from him, and half of the pages end out torn and covered with sweaty thumbprints. It's a bad habit, and he ought to grow out of it. They won't let him treat the Bible like that.

'LEO!' I said because when people are reading, you have to shout at them as though you're waking them up. 'LEO!'

He jolted and stared up at me with his big noble religious eyes, still hanging onto the book, which I noticed was called *The Marvellous Deeds of Father Damien Amongst the Lepers*.

'What?' he said, looking shocked and you would be, reading that.

I don't beat around the bush, so I said, 'How did your dad get to be so rich?'

Leo tugged his chin just like I'm sure a priest would, although a priest might have a beard, and went, 'Hmmmm. He's in business,' he said at last, as though it were a revelation.

Leo looks so intelligent. Perhaps it's true that looks deceive.

I sighed impatiently. 'What sort of business?' After all, my father was in business, and he wasn't rich. There had to be more to it than just being in business.

'Um, I don't know, really,' said Leo, as if he'd never actually thought about it.

'Well, how did he start out?' I demanded. He must know something. 'Doesn't he ever tell stories about the olden days when he was poor as a mouse, how he got his lucky break?' And they would be very olden olden days, because remember Leo's father is eighty-two.

Leo brightened up a bit. 'He told me once when he was starving to death he sold a story to a magazine.'

'A story?' Now I was the one frowning. 'What do you mean, a story?'

But Leo didn't know what sort of story. He didn't even

73

know what sort of magazine. He didn't know anything.

'All I know is his brother never spoke to him again,' said Leo solemnly.

I grunted and turned my back on him. A story. He sold a story to a magazine ... Perhaps it wasn't such a bad idea. After all, I had a story – the one I wrote about Calx the Cactus. It was still in my pocket, carefully folded up, as I had forgotten to put my uniform in the wash, which was just as well, because if I had remembered it would be a ball of mushed-up ink and paper by now.

I left Leo with the marvels of Father Damien, and went and sat down on a bench on the other side of the playground. I reached into my pocket, pulled it out and unfolded it. 'Calx the Cactus'. Three whole pages. As I reread it, I couldn't help but be impressed. I remembered how our teacher had told me once I was a 'natural writer' – it's true, she tells everyone that because she likes to be encouraging, but what if with me she really meant it? Couldn't I sell this story to a magazine and become rich like Leo's father?

I folded 'Calx the Cactus' up again and put it back in my pocket. Now, in business, you have to act quickly, my father says, before anyone realises what you're doing. I had to find the name and address of a magazine and send off my story straight away. So that afternoon when the bell went, I got hold of Griselda (at least I didn't have to worry about looking out for the Lego Lady any more, seeing she knew where we lived already) and pulled her down a side street.

'We've got to stop at the newspaper stand,' I told her.

'Why?' whined Griselda, and 'I'm STARVING!' because she knows the newspaper stand also sells lollipops and bubblegum.

'I don't have any money,' I said, dashing her hopes. 'I've just got to look at something.'

'I'm too tired to walk any more!' wailed Griselda. 'I'm EXHAUSTED.'

The newspaper stand is one of those little kiosks that is covered, absolutely covered, with newspapers and magazines, and if you look very hard you can actually see someone sitting right in the middle of them all who takes your money. Not that I ever buy newspapers, but sometimes I go along with Alaric whose mother always gives him lots of money in case he falls down a ravine on the way home from school. I don't know what he'd do with the money if he did fall down a ravine, but what he usually does is buy butterscotch which he shares with me.

Now today, as I said, I had no money at all, but I didn't want the newspaper-seller to know that. So I took out my little wallet (which is a nice crimson leather one that Abigail gave me for my birthday) and I peered right in amongst all the bits of print and sugar and found the small man in the middle and I said, 'I want a copy of a magazine with stories in it.'

Well, the way he jumped on his stool and stared at me, anyone would think I'd asked for something positively disgusting and he's got plenty of magazines like that for sale, I can tell you.

'What?' he said in a kind of a throaty gurgle.

I took a cool breath and repeated my question. 'Could you please give me a copy of a magazine that has stories in it SHUT UP GRISELDA!' because she was going on about how hungry she was and pointing at the packets of jelly beans which happened to coincide with the height of her nose.

I suppose the newspaper-selling man wanted to get rid of me quickly in case he got a reputation for dealing with minors – which means children, not people who dig for coal, by the way – because he got up off his stool and poked about disdainfully amongst the great piles, muttering away 'stories, stories, stories' until I thought I would go MAD.

'Here!' he said at last, 'try that.' He tossed over a thickish thing with an orange cover and big grey letters typed across it. Pretending to be very learned I leaned on the tower of afternoon newspapers and flipped through it – all that tiny grey writing and not one picture!

What I was looking for, of course, was an address, a little square like in the Sunday comics that says: 'We pay for your jokes and stories, just send them to:' That kind of thing. I looked and I looked and Griselda was going bananas and so was the selling man, I could tell and he said, 'Well, come on, girlie!' and everyone knows you shouldn't call people that!

I turned back to the front of the magazine very crossly indeed and there was the address – right next to how much it cost to subscribe, which made me feel quite faint.

All I can say is these literary types must make a lot of money if they can afford those prices. I whipped out a leaky pen from my pocket and scribbled the address on Griselda's hand because mine was already written all over with black triangles from last week's geometry lesson and the man said, 'What are you doing?' and I said airily, 'Oh, I've already read this one. I was hoping for the new edition,' and I dropped the magazine and Griselda and I ran and ran and I won't be going back there for butterscotch for a while I can tell you.

chapter thirteen

. . . I POST AN IMPORTANT DOCUMENT . . .

Now home is usually a refuge and a haven, but not for me, not any more. It was a place of torture. I spent every minute listening out for noises that might be Mimi returning. But she didn't return – not that evening, anyway. I supposed she was playing cat and mouse, as they say in the movies – you know, purring loudly outside the door, pretending to be about to pounce, and then just walking away. Waiting until you're off-guard and then springing for the kill.

I stayed up late copying out 'Calx The Cactus' in my neatest writing. I printed, because no one can ever read my running writing, and that might put my story at a disadvantage. I added a few illustrations, not that I am much good at drawing, but cactuses are fairly easy, just a blob or two with sticky bits coming out of it. I know there weren't any pictures in that magazine, but I think people like pictures in stories, don't you?

I wrote a letter to go with it.

Dear Sir, (I had this feeling the Editor would be a man)

Here is my story for publication in your next edition. Please send the money to me at the address below as soon as possible, in cash.

Thank you.

Yours, Anupam.

I decided that 'Anupam' would be my pen name.

A pen name is a pretend name that authors use if their real name isn't very appealing. Let's face it, 'Anupam', meaning 'beyond compare', is better than 'Claudia', meaning 'clubfooted'. I didn't doubt for a moment that the editor of the magazine would be fluent in both Sanskrit and Latin – if he wasn't, who would be?

I also put Anupam's address – for safety. I could just imagine the letter full of money coming and my father picking it up and saying 'Anupam – Anupam – there's no Anupam here!' and tossing it in the garbage disposal unit.

I managed to get hold of Griselda's hand in the bath in the nick of time – she's mad about washing, even though everyone knows it's unenvironmental. I wrote the address of the magazine on an envelope and stuck on two stamps to make sure it arrived quickly. On the top I added in red ink 'Strictly Confidential', because nobody can resist opening a letter with that on it, can they? I've noticed when my father gets a letter like that he opens it very quickly and turns pale and has to sit down on the sofa at once. I rather liked the thought of the editor opening my letter and turning pale and sitting down on the sofa.

I took the letter with me next morning as Griselda and I walked to school. It was a thick exciting package; I would have loved to have been on the receiving end of it myself. On the way we passed the postbox on the corner, and I kissed the back of it for luck and pushed it in the slot. Griselda was staring at me and she said, 'You'll get germs.'

'You're Neurotic,' I replied.

'I'm very Neurotic,' she corrected me, because even if she doesn't know what it means, she wants to be an extreme case. 'I want to join the recorder band.'

At school I told Anupam about it, more or less. I didn't actually tell her I'd sent my story to a magazine because that's not her type of thing, but I told her a letter would come to her house addressed to her but not to open it because it was actually for me.

'How will I know it's not for me?' asked Anupam, annoyingly, after I explained it about eight times.

'Do you ever get any letters?' I pointed out, not very kindly.

'Not so far,' she had to confess, 'but one day I might.'

'If you get a letter, just bring it in, will you!' I snapped.

'What if my parents ask who it's from?' said Anupam.

'Don't you dare open it!' I said quickly, seeing where this was leading. 'It's private! Strictly confidential.'

I suppose really I should have been nicer to her, seeing she was the one doing me the favour, but that's the artistic temperament for you. She's a pretty peaceful kind of person, anyway, and after a bit of huffiness she forgot all about it and offered me a bit of crumbled pink meringue. It was rather wet but I am not neurotic and found it very tasty.

Then I just had to wait. And wait. And wait.

chapter fourteen

. . . WAITING . . .

Waiting is terrible. Old people like my parents think nothing of waiting – they say things like 'Hasn't this week flashed by!' Well, I've never noticed a week flashing by – each week drags on and on and on in its own dreary meaningless way.

I had it all worked out. I sent the letter on Tuesday morning. The editor would get it on Wednesday. He would send the money that afternoon. Then Anupam would get it on Thursday and on Friday she would bring it in to school. So I just had to wait till Friday. Well, that was the theory . . .

I waited and I suffered. The days and the nights crawled by. My nerves were like marbles clattering on the floor. At school it was not so bad, as there were distractions, but at home I was on edge, any minute expecting Mimi to come banging on the door again.

I recalled those dreadful lines in green texta, and those three fearful kisses. It made me shiver. What was she doing out there – what was she planning? I had the RIGOURS, which means you go hot and cold and hot and cold and hot and cold and it's awful. I kept putting on jumpers and taking them off again.

My father, on the other hand, wasn't showing any particular signs of tension or desperation. If anything, he seemed a little more cheerful than usual. Once, he nearly turned off the television. He even began whistling – he can whistle the entire score of *Les Miserables*, but don't ask him to because it's extremely long. He and my mother murmured a lot in bed at night – whisper, whisper, whisper. Griselda played the recorder. To my horror, Mr Tolty had told my mother that Griselda had musical aptitude, so that's what happens when you put yourself in the hands of an expert.

I waited and I worried. After all, I didn't really know how much I would get paid for my story – what if it wasn't enough for Mimi? Maybe in the olden days when Leo's father was young and there wasn't any television, people paid more for stories than nowadays. I asked my father, 'Have you ever met any writers?'

He looked shifty for some reason and said, 'I've known a few.'

'How much money do they make?'

'Depends, I suppose,' replied my father. 'What sort of writer are you talking about?'

'Someone high class,' I replied with a cough. 'You

know, like Shakespeare,' because my father doesn't read much.

'I've never met anyone like Shakespeare,' said my father, very definitely indeed.

This was Thursday afternoon. My mother was out, and Griselda had gone to Winsome's, with her recorder, thank heavens. (Winsome's mother wouldn't let her come to our place any more.)

To calm my nerves, I did a bit of cooking. Despite my unceasing RIGOURS, I managed to make some Cornflake kisses, which don't need flour anyway, just lots of Corn-flakes and honey and melted margarine. Eventually my father wandered into the kitchen to see what I was doing.

'Have a Cornflake kiss,' I offered him, holding one up in my rather sticky fingers because I couldn't find any of those little paper containers to put them in.

'Um, no thanks,' he said, stepping back quickly. 'Run down to Peter's shop, will you, and get some butter and jam? And buy yourself an ice cream.'

Peter's shop is the general store nearest us. It is nice and clean and full of interesting things, not like that dark den of iniquity (which means evil goings-on) that I'd been forced to take refuge in with Griselda and Winsome that time.

'Great,' I said, snatching the money, desperate to do something, anything – although really I should have stayed there to protect him. Then my father added casually, 'Take your time. Go to the park or something.'

Out I ran into that surprisingly hot day, down to

Peter's shop. Hanging around outside the shop were some boys I know from martial arts class. I used to go every Friday night to martial arts until our teacher fell in love with a beautiful Black Belt with long blonde hair and ran away with her to the South Seas.

Now, as you know, apart from Alaric I'm not that keen on boys, but if you've spent hours and hours on the floor strangling each other every Friday night, you develop a kind of closeness, if you know what I mean. I didn't mind these boys, even though they're in the high school now and they've all shaved their hair off so they don't look at all attractive but at least you know they don't have nits.

They were hanging around the garbage bin and eating ice-creams in the shape of cowboys' faces with a big round piece of bubble gum for the nose. It's not nice to feel left out so I went in and bought one for myself.

We kind of ambled on from the garbage bin down to the park where the boys smoked cigarettes and pushed me on the swing and shouted at the stray dogs and kicked the toilet walls. Then we had a bit of a wrestle and a strangle in seven positions for old times' sake and then they said, 'Got to go. Dinner,' because boys do anything for food. We all bowed to each other in the Korean way just like our instructor taught us before he fell in love with the beautiful black belt. I went back to Peter's shop and bought some margarine and a very small jar of jam that came all the way from Lebanon because that ice-cream had been expensive.

When I slipped myself back in our front door I suppose at least an hour had passed. Griselda and my mother were still out. My father jumped up from the sofa, grinning, healthy and alive. He lunged over and kissed me and said, 'Things are looking up, Claudie my love, they're definitely looking up!'

Poor foolish man. I suppose he'd just been reading his horoscope in the paper which told him he would meet a dark stranger and have an overseas trip.

I felt quite hungry, in spite of the ice-cream. Living on a razor's edge takes its toll on your natural functions. I went into the kitchen, remembering my Cornflake kisses.

But I was too late. I found the plate, not in the fridge but on the kitchen bench, gleaming and entirely empty, next to a couple of dirty teacups.

Someone had got there before me, and licked the platter clean.

chapter fifteen

. . . I PUT INTO ACTION A BOLD PLAN,
NEARLY FOILED BY GRISELDA . . .

Friday morning. D-Day. The day I would get my money.

It was a terrible trip to school. Griselda insisted on playing her recorder all the way. I kept hoping someone might throw a stone out the window at her, or even turn the hose on her, because quite a few people were in their front yards watering their spiky flowers (in our neighbourhood spiky flowers are very popular in the front to keep the burglars out). But all the garden-waterers just smiled at her and her bilious hair and one madman even stood by his cactus, clapping.

When we finally reached the playground I ran to find Anupam. She was sitting as usual on the chairs outside the classroom. This is where she always waits for the bell, because she doesn't like getting dirty. She is the cleanest person on earth, beyond compare, let's face it.

'Hi!' she said, swinging her legs up and down. 'Do you like my new socks?'

'Where's the letter?' I demanded, not even glancing at the socks, although I must have a little bit because I remember they were black and yellow striped, like a bee.

'There wasn't any,' replied Anupam, peacefully.

I swayed. 'There must have been! Did you look?'

'There wasn't any,' Anupam repeated, those bumble-bee legs going up and down.

I sank onto a chair next to her, leaning on my bag, unfortunately squashing the banana my father had thoughtfully slipped into it that morning without telling me.

'Claudie!' shouted Abigail in my ear, jumping on me from behind. 'One of our puppies died.'

Well, she didn't look very upset.

'What happened?' I said, able to think of others even at the height of my own distress. I imagined the poor little lumpy dead thing snuggled up in the skirts of the mouldy White Queen.

'I suppose it was the Runt of the Litter,' said Anupan, swinging, tranquil as ever.

'Its number was up,' agreed Abigail.

Well, there are certainly a lot of philosophical people in the world, aren't there? I hope neither of those two ever become mothers. But what did I care for the dead puppies of the world, when it came down to it. I had my own concerns.

No letter. No money. Mimi. XXX.

'What am I going to do?' I wailed and burst into tears and then Abigail and Anupam and Alaric all crowded around me and gave me big hugs and I told them all about how I'd sent off the story and I needed the money desperately because of Mimi XXX and WHAT WAS I GOING TO DO?

Well, my friends are very practical. They let me sob a bit and then a little bit more and then they said that's enough and I don't know who suggested it first, but they said there was only one thing to do and they were right. I had to go into town where they made the magazine and explain the urgency of the situation to the editor and then he would give me the money straight away.

'Cash!' said Alaric decisively.

'You'll have to go today,' pointed out Abigail. 'Monday might be too late and offices aren't open on the weekends.'

'But how?' I began, ready for another wailing attack. They told me to be quiet and it would be all right, I could just sneak out of school while our teacher was reading a poem or something and they would cover for me.

Again that dreadful bell rang and in we filed. It was hot, hot, hot, and it shouldn't have been at that time of year, and more of our class than usual fell asleep at their desks. First we did maths, and a few of them were listening, but then we did handwriting and a few more dropped off, so by the time we were ready for Society and Culture only Cinnamon and I were left awake – even Leo was asleep, although he was sleeping with his eyes open, which is an off-putting sight, I can tell you.

But in the meantime, I was gathering strength. They were right – I mean Alaric and Abigail and Anupam. It's a dog-eat-dog world, my father always says, the survival of the fittest, the law of the jungle, the weak will be trampled into the earth, all that sort of thing. I bet all those Nobel Prize for Literature winners were as ruthless as Texan billionaires. I would go into that magazine and demand my money at once. On the double!

Then the bell rang for the morning break. Everyone woke up as though it was an alarm clock and tumbled out of their desks at a great pace except for Boaz, who is allowed to stay inside because he has delicate eyes. Every day he eats dry noodles – he will only eat foods that look like rubber bands. Dry noodles made a most peculiar sound when being eaten, rather like the crunching of very small bones.

I couldn't eat a thing. Outside, Alaric, Abigail and Anupam crowded about me like three Harpies and said, 'You're going to have to make a move.'

Well, one of them said it, they didn't say it all at once. Then Alaric said, 'Just pretend to be sick. That's what I always do. Tell the teacher you've got concussion.'

'Then she'll call an ambulance,' pointed out Anupam. 'Better just say you've got a little headache.'

'She'll just say, "join the club",' said Abigail with feeling, as she had tried this on our teacher a few times herself.

In the end, we decided I should say I had an abdominal migraine. There's something powerful about the word 'abdominal'. Then I could go to sick bay, and from there, sneak away. Now I suppose you think it's quite bad, this plan, and it's true, it was bad. But I have a bad streak, which I probably haven't mentioned so far. It's not my fault, I come from a bad family and they shouldn't have called me Claudia, they should have called me Patience, or Mercy or Charity.

When our teacher came in from the break, she said we were going to do Science. She adores Science – what she calls Science, anyway, which is all about weighing things and throwing heavy objects off high towers. That woman just asks for trouble.

So I put on a pale face and said, 'I've got an abdominal migraine, can I go to sick bay?'

Our teacher looked alarmed and said, 'Oh dear, yes, you'd better go quickly. Goodness me!'

'Sick bay' – well. In the boarding-school stories I read they have a whole hospital and an army of nurses to take your temperature every half hour, and someone called Matron who brings you dishes of dried apricots. In our school they have an old cane sofa near the canteen with some old, green cushions for you to crawl up into a ball onto, and if you are close to death they might ring your mother in case there are any last words she might want to note down. Still, just now that was exactly the kind of sick bay I needed.

I went over to the cane sofa and lay on it, my hand on my stomach. When anyone came near I started to pant heavily, so they shot me a frightened look and walked quickly past. People in my school believe in looking after Number One, although I don't think that's a Core Value.

I waited until the school became very quiet again, when everyone was in their classrooms snoozing away and all the teachers were waving things about desperately in front of them. The canteen ladies were all busy making cheese sandwiches and cutting up frozen oranges, pretending that they are as delicious as ice-creams, which they are not, and our Principal was deep in thought behind the brown door.

Then very, very quietly, I got up from my sick bed and walked away. The floors in our school are made from shiny rubber and they squeak, so I had to tread very carefully. I am good at this, actually, I should be a cat burglar, which doesn't mean someone who goes around stealing cats, as I used to think, by the way.

I headed towards the front gates of the school. They are enormous and historic, in memory of a noble pioneer who lived here in days of yore. Outside the gates, just along the road a bit, I knew there was a bus-stop that led into the city, and the city was where the office of the magazine was.

So I was slinking up towards the gates and my hands were about to thrust them open and burst out into freedom when, 'CLAUDIE!!!'

chapter sixteen

I swung around.

Griselda! Standing there behind me, all by herself, her mouth dropping open.

'What are you doing here?' I hissed.

'We're drawing trees,' said Griselda, waving a white sheet of paper. 'But I lost my charcoal.'

Wouldn't you know it, Griselda's class was out there in the playground, drawing trees! I squinted into the distance. They were sitting here and there, scribbling their mad little drawings. If there was ever a day in the history of the world that children should not be out in the blazing sunshine it was that day.

If I was mentally disturbed, I might have said to myself, 'Just my luck, nothing ever goes right for me!' But Alaric's psychologist says that such reasoning is the product of a sick mind, and he should know. So instead I said to myself, 'What joy! Dear little Griselda,' but I suppose I must have been baring my teeth in a not terribly friendly manner because Griselda's eyes filled with tears and I could see she was about to scream, which would cook my goose, so I smiled (it was hard, but I did) and said, 'Come on, Griz, come with me into town!'

I reached out for her hand, which I noticed, unfortunately too late, was absolutely black with dusty charcoal.

'Into town?' she repeated doubtfully, because although Griselda also comes from a bad family she is a goody-goody and they do say there is a freak in every generation.

'Yes, I've got an appointment,' I said, which sounded like a dentist and that seemed to convince her but then she said, 'What will Mr Igloo say?'

She meant her teacher. His name is really not Mr Igloo, it is Mr Ingall but she is backward.

'Oh do come on, Grizzle, I'm running late,' I snapped, tugging her grubby little hand and she was brave for her (she is my sister after all) and wiped away her tears with her other hand which put charcoal dust all across her face so she looked like a chimney sweep. As she did so she let go of her picture of a tree (as if anyone would know that's what it was, it looked more like a small intestine) and a gust of hot wind blew it away and into the oncoming traffic.

'You have to come now,' I said, as she looked tragically at her disappearing work of art. 'Otherwise you'll get in trouble.'

She couldn't argue with that, so she came. And even though I might complain about her, in a secret sort of way I was quite glad to have her with me, because the truth was I was just a bit nervous about the whole thing.

When we got on the bus I realised I didn't have any money – I am not much of a forward planner. But I am good in an emergency, and I explained to the bus driver, 'We lost our bus passes and I'm having a major tooth extraction.'

The bus driver couldn't have looked more bored and made a kind of grunt that meant, I suppose, 'Get up the back and leave me alone.'

So we sat right up the back on the big seat. The bus wasn't crowded as it was the middle of the day. We sat up on our knees and looked out the rear window and I'm afraid Griselda waved at people in cars in her bilious way and some of them even waved back.

Our school is not that far from the city, about twenty minutes down a big highway. I knew when we were getting into the city because all the buildings began growing taller and there were even more cars and buses and I saw the edge of a big park where we had been one holidays to taste medieval food, which I don't recommend. I had no idea where to get off, but I wasn't about to tell Griselda that, so I just waited until we came to a place where lots and lots of people were getting off and we did too, which just as well as it was actually the final stop.

As the bus drove away, Griselda and I stood on the city street feeling very small amongst all those buildings and people and cars. At least I felt small, and Griselda is smaller than me. I suddenly realised I did not in fact have the address of the magazine with me, so it's just as well Griselda was there because she still had it written on her hand, in spite of the bath. I must have used one of those indelible pens which it's no use washing, you just have to wait until your skin wears away.

There it was, still legible – 22 Leopold Street. All I had to do was ask where Leopold Street was. Pulling Griselda along, (she was so overawed by where she was that she'd forgotten how to talk) we went inside a kind of arcade that was unfortunately full of food shops. I say unfortunately because it was about lunch time and I didn't have any money and the food looked so delicious – cakes and pies and ice-creams – even the vegetable soup looked slightly delicious which shows how hungry I must have been. And of course Griselda recovered her powers of speech alas and whined out, 'I'm STARVING to death!' And she went and pressed her nose against the glass of a donut counter. But in the city people are not so susceptible to bilious hair and nobody said, 'Oh you dear little girl, here, have one for nothing'. Instead the man behind the counter said, 'Move on if you're not buying anything,' which could be a motto for life, couldn't it? In this dog-eat-dog jungle of a world.

So we moved on, and I was looking for the sort of person I could ask where Leopold Street was, but no one would catch my eye – I suppose they might have thought I was a drug dealer because I do look a bit depraved. The only person who smiled at me was a strange old man with thin long hair who was standing in one spot and swaying to and fro reading from the Book of Jeremiah – I know that because it was written on a card at his feet. 'Today's Reading Is From the Book of Jeremiah.'

I was so desperate I was almost going to ask him when Griselda, proving herself useful yet again, said, 'Can I play with that!'

She was pointing at a nearby plastic screen with lots of little red lights that lit up when you pressed a button, and I realised it was an electronic map.

Griselda entertained herself pressing buttons on the map and I had a good look at all the streets. I like maps – we used to do lots of map reading at school, walking around the real streets following routes until one day a man in a woollen hat approached our teacher in the Daryl Jackson Gardens and said some perverse things. Anyway, I was confident I would find Leopold Street and at last I did, and it wasn't really too far from the little red light that said: 'YOU ARE HERE'.

'Aha!' I said, very pleased. 'There it is! Come on, Griselda.'

We left the arcade and headed for Leopold Street. Now we saw a lot of interesting things on the way, but for artistic reasons I won't list absolutely everything which is what Leo does when we have to write about what we did on our trip to the Science Museum – I mean, let's face it, nobody's interested in how many steps it took from the trilobite hall to the insect pavillion, and how there was a spelling mistake in the sign above the Sabre-Toothed Tiger.

So I'll just mention the woman who was playing the national anthem on the violin which is not the right instrument for it, the man walking around with a tin of strawberry jam tied around his neck and the chocolate shop as big as a supermarket – now that was something! Griselda and I took a basket and went to all the different booths where you dished out your own chocolates – white and brown and pink – into little tubs and we dished out tonnes and tonnes and had a few samples, because we didn't know if we would like them, did we? And then we waited until there was a big line at the check-out and we dumped our basket and ran for it.

How hot it was out there! Luckily we found a fountain that was like a great wall of freezing water – I know it was freezing because I washed Griselda's hand and face in it so she would look respectable for the editor.

Unfortunately she screamed and everyone stared at me. But then Griselda put her head down in the water and took a great mouthful of it and swished it around her mouth and spat it out and so everyone stared at her instead.

'We're going to the dentist and I've been eating chocolate,' she explained to anyone who was listening.

'That's not very clean, you know, dear,' said someone at last. It was a man in a uniform and I nearly died but it wasn't the police. It was a red uniform, with 'Security' written on the shoulder.

'Can you direct us to Leopold Street?' I said, grabbing the chance – I am good at that. I spoke very quickly because I didn't want Griselda to hear about the water not being clean, she being neurotic about germs.

'Leopold Street. Ah.'

He ahed and he ahed – someone was probably robbing a bank right at that moment, but he seemed to have all the time in the world. In the end he beckoned another security guard called Frank. Frank at least had some kind of brain and he said, 'Just go up the steps and turn left.'

And that's exactly what we did.

chapter seventeen

. . . I COME FACE TO FACE . . .

We went up the stairs and we turned left and there we found Leopold Street. It wasn't much of a street – more a weedy little alley – and it was dark because the buildings on either side were like tall walls. I didn't think it was a very suitable place for a magazine – they must hardly ever get any visitors. If I was the editor I would have my office at the beach next to an ice-cream parlour or a fish-and-chip shop. It might be windy, but everyone likes the beach.

Griselda pulled on my arm and wailed, 'I don't want to go!' and I said, 'We'll get some lunch when we get there.' I don't think there's anything wrong with telling someone a lie to get them through life's difficult patches, do you? It worked, anyway, and she came trotting after me, though I think I was as scared as she was.

'Look for number 2 and 2,' I said, because she knows the number two, if nothing else.

We walked down slowly, looking for numbers, which were not easy to see in the dark grime. There was a funny little shop that sold fans, and another one with computer parts in the window, and then there was a restaurant with a hanging sign. It was a picture of a bullfighter and the words, COME IN FOR SUCKLING PIG.

No thanks very much! You couldn't see inside, but there was a lot of noise coming out of it, and I supposed it was full of toreadors (that's Spanish for bullfighters) ripping the flesh off a suckling pig and shoving it into their mouths.

'That place smells funny,' Griselda remarked as we hurried by, and I said, 'Well, hold your nose, then!'

'That's it!' shouted Griselda, sounding very strange, because she was pointing with one hand and holding her nose with the other. 'A two and a two!'

And it was. 22. This was 22 Leopold Street. I felt shaky, how great opera singers must feel, I suppose, as they're waiting in the wings about to burst onto stage to make everyone gasp in awe.

'So it is,' I replied calmly, although horribly nervous. 'Take your hand from your nose, Griselda dear, and let us enter.'

I spoke this way to get me in the mood to ask for my money. Griselda, who wasn't used to my more gracious manner, dropped her hand from her nose in shock. Meekly, she stood next to me at the locked door of number 22.

There was no knocker, just an electrical bell with one

of those little loudspeakers you have to shout into to say who it is. We don't have one at home – my father always says nothing beats a good old-fashioned peephole.

I pressed on the buzzer. Surprisingly, it didn't buzz at all but played 'Happy Birthday To You', and a song like that you can't help singing along to, so we did. Then I told Griselda to shush, so we could hear the editor's voice when it finished.

But there was nothing. Silence. Surely he couldn't be out. I pressed the buzzer again, and this time it wasn't 'Happy Birthday To You' but 'Home on the Range' which both Griselda and I happen to know, because we had to sing it for the parents at the last Education Week.

Where never is heard
A discouraging word!
And the skies are not cloudy all day!

We sang until the end, and Griselda even made a few lonely howling dog noises. Then we waited for the voice. It was rather tense. Still nothing.

I was just about to put my finger to the buzzer for the third time and see which song came out ('Little Brown Jug' perhaps, or 'We wish you a merry Christmas') when a VOICE cried out at us out of the loud speaker, reminding me uncomfortably of our Principal.

'WHO'S THERE?' and I said, with not a moment's hesitation, 'The author of "Calx The Cactus"!' and there was a silence. I suppose it might have been a stunned silence, although that's hard to tell through an intercom.

Then the voice said, 'WHO?'

'One of your contributors!' I bellowed back and some people coming out of the Suckling Pig restaurant looked at us strangely and I started to feel hot and uncomfortable, which is not how I wanted to feel, so I said, as firmly as I could, 'PLEASE LET US IN NOW!'

Silence. If this was the editor, he either had bad manners or was a deep thinker. No more words came out, but there was that funny 'zzzz' sound that some doors make when the person inside is releasing the lock and you have to push very hard. We pushed and we pushed because it was so heavy, like the door of a mental asylum, I thought, not that I would know.

When we finally got it open, I fully expected to see the editor on the other side of it, but there was no one there – just a stairway, very narrow, going up, up, up. There was nowhere else to go and the door slammed heavily behind us, so we couldn't get out again.

I said to Griselda, 'Well, come on then.'

'I'm tired!' began Griselda, 'I'm ex . . .' but I started up the stairs and she came dribbling after me, whingeing all the way. I suppose even Shakespeare might have been embarrassed by his family.

We climbed up past a couple of little windows – so small they might have been made for a prison – and we kept on going because, as I said, we couldn't go back and at last we reached the top and there was a door.

'This must be it!' I whispered to Griselda in great excitement. 'Now be good!'

I pushed this door open without knocking because he

knew we were coming, didn't he, and I didn't want to give the impression of TIMIDITY because everyone knows all the best writers are bold and confronting.

I pushed it open, and –

chapter eighteen

. . . WITH THE EDITOR HIMSELF, WHO IS
NOT ALL HE IS CRACKED UP TO BE . . .

'Oh!'

That wasn't me, that was him. The Editor.

At least I had to assume he was the editor, although
he didn't have a pencil stuck behind his ear. He had a
mane, a positive mane of grey and brown hair and he
was dressed in a dark green suit and a pale yellow tie
and he had wild eyes.

'Hallo there!' I said, quaking.

'Can I help you?' said the Editor, not exactly coming
forward.

'Yes, well, yes.'

Griselda said, 'Are you going to give us chewing
gum?' because, of course, she thought the Editor was the
dentist and our dentist always gives us chewing gum at
the end.

'Oh, er,' said the Editor, staring down at Griselda, and she is rather low.

'Where do I sit?' asked Griselda, looking around the room, which was large and bare and filled with grey metal filing cabinets. 'I'll go first.'

Griselda ALWAYS goes first, and everyone lets her and it's really not fair – then I suddenly remembered we weren't at the dentist and I looked the Editor straight in the eye, which wasn't so easy because, as I said before, his eyes were WILD and I said, 'I am the author of "Calx the Cactus"!'

This announcement (and it was the second time) didn't quite have the effect I imagined. I thought his face would clear and he would smile and shake my hand and say, what an honour, how delightful, how much can I pay you – things like that.

But he looked more puzzled, if anything, almost as though he didn't know what I was talking about.

'Oh yes,' he said, looking around, hoping perhaps that someone else would step forward from the shadows and help him out. But there was nobody there – there weren't even any shadows. This place was wide and open like a furniture shop. I prefer a few corridors and closed doors, myself.

'Ah, what can I do for you two ... dear ... little ... girls ...' each word coming out very slowly and uncertainly, as though he was afraid we might not be two dear little girls after all, which we're not.

'I am "Anupam!"' I said.

106

Perhaps this would enlighten him.

'No you're not,' whispered Griselda, thinking I might have got amnesia, 'you're Claudie.'

'My pen name,' I continued grandly, 'is "Anupam". I sent you my story, "Calx the Cactus".'

The wild eyes of the Editor suddenly became shifty and his feet started to shuffle and he said, 'Oh, yes, well . . . very busy . . . you know . . . so much paper comes across my desk . . . all too much really . . . very nice . . .'

He stopped mid-sentence and added with a frown, 'You're a little young, aren't you.'

'Oh, you have to start young these days,' I told him confidently. 'Otherwise you haven't got a chance.'

'Oh.' He looked taken aback. 'Yes, well, nice to meet you and er . . .'

He was making movements with his hands towards the door as though we were a pair of cats! Well, if that's how he treated his other authors, I'm FLABBERGASTED he's got any contributors at all. And I wasn't moving anyway, not until I got my money. I had my family to save, after all.

'But!' I interrupted, keeping my feet firmly on the carpet and carefully not looking at Griselda who was now lying on the floor talking to a piece of fluff. 'What about my story?'

I gave him my fiercest face, which I've noticed puts a lot of people off. He seemed to get the idea because he changed tactics and he said, 'Would you like a drink, um? It's a hot day, isn't it?'

He motioned towards the teeny tiny little fridge in the corner, and my heart sank, because my father told me you can always tell how well a business is doing by the size and quality of their white goods. (That means fridges and washing machines, but you wouldn't expect a magazine to have a washing machine, would you?) By the looks of the poor little fridge, this magazine was just about bankrupt.

'I want some cordigal!' demanded Griselda, standing up. She meant cordial – she just has to throw a 'g' into everything. She shook her bilious hair at the Editor and he smiled in that pathetic way they all do and murmured uncertainly, 'There might be a scrap of milk . . .'

He opened the fridge and what a smell! I nearly fainted. He reached into the back, found an open carton and showed it to me. At the bottom of the carton lay something yellow and globby like plasticine. I said, 'Drink that, and die!'

I don't suppose he wanted us lying dead on the floor – he didn't want us there in the peak of health, if you ask me. So he put the carton back in the fridge and poured us each a glass of water. Then he found a tin of biscuits with currants in them that looked like they dated back to the Bible. I believe some artistic types don't notice what they eat and drink, but I am not one of them. I have natural animal appetites.

'Um. Sit down,' said the Editor, waving vaguely at some chairs and a huge desk near the window.

So we sat down around his desk and there were bits

of paper everywhere and paper clips and pencils and things like that and nowhere did I see any signs of my story or my envelope or anything. Then Griselda pointed at a glass ink well and said, 'I saw one of those in a museum once.'

Well, that's not much of a conversation starter. I wanted to get down to business, but I had to get on his good side first, so I dipped my biscuit in my glass of water (which was a mistake because the biscuit immediately disintegrated and sank down to the bottom) and I pointed at a photograph on the wall and I said, 'Who's that?'

Well, that got him going. He stood up and went into this long speech about whoever it was and whenever it was and why it was and why it was so important for whatever it was and on and on and on he went and he marched up and down the dusty old floor positively DECLAIMING. It's a pity I don't remember anything he said because I suppose it might have been useful in later life, when I start mixing in literary circles once I'm a Baroness. But I'm afraid I was a bit distracted trying to rescue the remains of my biscuit from the bottom of my glass and I had to stick my fingers right inside and unfortunately my fingers weren't all that clean and the water took on a grey-brown colour and all the dried (very dried) currants floated to the top.

Then Griselda said, 'I am the best in my class at hanging upside-down,' and she is, but you shouldn't boast, should you? and obviously the Editor thought so too because he stopped talking and gave her a VERY peculiar look indeed. Then he said to me, 'But you, as a young writer – now what did you say your story was about?'

'It's about a cactus,' I said, licking my fingers and standing up because he was beckoning to me to go and join him at the window.

'About a cactus,' he repeated solemnly. 'A cactus. I hope you don't mind my saying, my dear, that's a mistake.'

A mistake! My heart sank. My heart sank and my gorge rose. (That's in Shakespeare.).

But the Editor didn't notice my emotional state. Actually, he wasn't a very sensitive man. He threw open the window.

'Lean right out and look!' he commanded.

I got nervous because it crossed my mind that he might be a homicidal maniac and he was going to push me out the window and I would land right in the middle of all those carniverous toreadors gobbling down the suckling pig and that's not the way to end your life, is it? I tried to EXTRICATE myself, which means get away, but he started talking again, grasping my shoulder.

'Out there!' he cried, pointing grandly. 'There is the material for your fiction!'

I peered out, standing on tiptoes, looking where he pointed. Perhaps he had an interesting neighbour who might be a good character in a book, like a hunchback or a wizened old washerwoman. But all he was pointing

110

at was the city – actually, he had quite a good view. If his magazine went out of business, (and that was more than likely, I'm afraid) he could open a revolving restaurant.

'There!' he repeated. 'Look there for your stories – there! Not ... er ... in the succulent garden.' (Succulent is an uncomplimentary word for a cactus.)

I shook my head firmly, stood back from the window and looked down.

'I don't think so. I don't like cars.'

'Not cars!' The Editor tossed back his mane in horror. 'Life! Life!'

I was looking down. Down at something horrible.

'Well, cactuses are alive,' I mumbled, but I could hardly get the words out.

I was looking down into the wastepaper basket.

'Cactuses are prickly.' That was Griselda's contribution, but I scarcely heard her.

'Life!' The Editor repeated. 'Write from Life!'

I was looking down into the wastepaper basket straight at my copy of 'Calx the Cactus'.

In the wastepaper basket. He had opened the letter, I suppose I should have been grateful for that much. But he had opened it only to toss it straight into the dust heap. And forgotten all about it.

'Have you considered poetry?' asked the Editor, thinking, I suppose, that one could write a poem, at least, about a cactus, if I insisted on being so pig-headed.

I was DEVASTATED. I was OUTRAGED. I saw my

life in tatters before me. I saw Mimi with a club bludgeoning my father to death, leaving three large XXXs on the mirror in green lipstick.

'Well,' I said, hoarsely, 'I suppose poems are short.'

The Editor, not being an artist himself, so not knowing that you have to be practical in these matters, coughed – well, just about choked – and then he said, 'Short! but SUBLIME!'

Well, I didn't know what sublime meant and I still don't if you want the truth, but Griselda heard the last bit and she perked up from where she was on the floor scratching her initials in the desk with a pair of scissors (she can't write, but she knows a few letters which she thinks are her name) and shouted in that very particular way of hers, 'I WANT SOME LIME CORDIGAL!'

I had to get out of there. I was about to burst into tears, and I am not the emotional type.

'We have to go now. Thank you for the refreshments,' I said rapidly, grabbing Griselda.

The Editor smiled, a lovely smile, the way people do when they're relieved that their guest is leaving at last. He reached over to shake our hands just like my father says you should, even if the deal falls through, but my hand was wet with sweat and I was trembling. I suppose he must have noticed.

'Oh dear, have I hurt your feelings?' he said, helplessly – well, nobody likes a weeping child in their office.

You could see he didn't know what to do – he obviously

didn't have a piece of chocolate to take my mind off my problems, but he tried what I suppose he thought was the next best thing. He spun around to the bookshelf behind him, scanned the rows of books wildly looking for something suitable, then finally pulled out a big black book as thick as the Bible.

'Let me present you with this,' he said, rather formally, thrusting the book into my hands. 'You wish to be a writer? Take this as your model!'

I stared at the book. It was wobbly, because of the tears, but I could see that at least it wasn't the Bible. I read the words on the cover: *THE UNCONSOLED.*

'Um, thanks,' I said, briefly, sniffing hard, because you have to be polite, don't you? But what a terrible title! I certainly wasn't going to waste my time reading that.

'Your shoelaces are undone,' observed Griselda helpfully to the Editor who nodded vaguely and said, 'Er . . . yes . . . thank you.'

'In my school you can't leave kindergarten until you know how to tie your shoelaces,' mentioned Griselda, which is a lie because then most of my class would still be in the kindergarten.

I tugged her on the arm. I had to get out of there, before he could thrust anything else into my hands.

The Editor stood in the middle of that room staring at us as though we were a vanishing APPARITION. Perhaps later he would come to think of us as a religious experience. He waved weakly, then pushed back his long

113

hair from his forehead. I pushed the door open, and dragged Griselda out with me.

BANG! It closed behind us and down the stairs we scuttled, down, down, round and down to that heavy outer door. I heaved it open (it's amazing how strong you can be when you're desperate), it groaned and squeaked, and out we bolted, into the city again.

chapter nineteen

. . . WE MAKE GOOD OUR ESCAPE BACK TO
SCHOOL WHERE NOBODY CARES IF I AM ALIVE
OR DEAD . . .

A traumatic experience like that is not something to be
shaken off lightly, but I am masterful, even in times of
bitter disappointment. I managed to get Griselda and me
a seat on the bus back to school without TOO much
trouble (there were a few difficulties with the bus driver,
but artistically speaking they are better omitted).

We got off the bus near school and I was feeling very
quiet and sad, not to mention full of dread. Griselda
luckily was too tired even to complain, thank goodness,
and we plodded silently together back to the school gates,
from which I had set out with such glorious hopes, now
nothing but ashes in my mouth.

Outside, there was an ambulance parked – I thought,
Oh no, our teacher has had a heart attack worrying about

where I am, and I did feel guilty because she is a nice woman who tries hard.

'Come on, Grizzel!' I said and we trotted over to the ambulance and took a look inside, but it wasn't my teacher at all. It was just Alaric (AGAIN!) doing another fainting turn and if they haven't learnt by now, they never will.

'Hallo Claudie! I got hit on the head by a bag of birdseed.' Alaric waved at me cheerfully, not remotely unconscious. 'Are you feeling better?' He winked at me meaningfully.

I suddenly remembered my abdominal migraine. I was about to put on my expression of extreme suffering, clutching my stomach, when we heard a voice crying, 'There she is!'

It was Mr Ingalls and with him our Principal! I could scarcely believe it, our Principal had actually emerged from his office – he must have really been worried about me! He still had his sunglasses on and now he also had an enormous sunhat. It's good to know he looks after himself, I suppose.

'Griselda! Where on earth did you get to? We've been having a man hunt!' said Mr Ingalls, and they couldn't have had a man hunt because Griselda's a girl and anyway, what about me, didn't anybody miss me?

I said quickly, 'We had an appointment in town, didn't Griselda give you the note from my mother?'

Griselda looked up at me and was about to open her big mouth but you remember my pinching technique?

She closed her mouth and scratched her ear instead.

'We thought she had an infestation,' I explained, inspirationally, 'so we had to take her to a specialist.'

Well, that got rid of our Principal, on the double. But Mr Ingalls, who is not frightened of insects or the Tower of Terror, according to Griselda, hmmphed at us, 'Come along then, back to class,' and he and Griselda also disappeared and the ambulance drove away with Alaric inside for another round of hospital tests and I went off sorrowfully alone, broken and alone.

In my classroom they were doing a performance of Boaz's story about the rubber bands, and if you can picture that, then you are a more creative spirit than I am. I slunk into my chair next to Anupam who looked at me hopefully but I wouldn't meet her eye so I supposed she guessed it had all been a disaster . . . Our teacher smiled at me as if she just possibly remembered who I was.

Abigail poked me in the back with a Texta colour.

'What happened?' she whispered, but I just shook my head and didn't turn around. I didn't want to talk about it, not right then.

'What's that?' asked Leo, pointing at my copy of THE UNCONSOLED and I snapped at once, 'It's mine and you can't touch it!' because Leo is one of those grasping people who are always on the lookout for cast-offs. Now maybe I didn't want the book but it's only natural that I didn't want anyone else to have it. And I also didn't want to watch Boaz's play because I was jealous and in a turmoil – and my father was doomed and it was all my fault – so I opened the book instead, pretending to read it.

I turned to the front page, and to my surprise, I saw that the book had actually been signed by the author! He had a very difficult name – I couldn't even spell it for you let alone pronounce it. His signature was good, though – it was very scrawly and messy and superior in black ink. I had never seen the signature of a real author before and I was impressed.

I got to thinking. I leaned over to Anupam's metal pencil case, picked a brown pen because brown is sophisticated, and underneath the author's signature I started practising my own. My real name, I mean, not "Anupam", as clearly the sacred tongue is completely wasted on magazine editors.

Boaz's play droned on and on – whoever thought rubber bands could say so much? – and I kept on practising my signature. Sometimes the tears came back into my eyes from somewhere or other and then I pressed very hard and deep with the pen. Soon the title page of the book was completely covered in brown ink so you couldn't really see the real author's signature any more, which was a bit of a pity for him I suppose.

Leo and Cinnamon were watching me, and they copied me of course, they got out bits of paper and started practising their own signatures which I'm afraid did not look sophisticated at all and anyone would know they were never going to become famous writers.

I kicked Leo's chair (not Cinnamon's, remember she's

an expert at Chinese burns) and hissed and I threw a spit-ball at him, which he deserved for copying but naturally he told our teacher. He said it was his duty because spit-balls are not hygienic and I might have whooping cough.

Our teacher was terribly cross for disturbing the play at its climax, although I don't know how you could tell, and she said she was going to do something really nasty to me, which was almost an exciting prospect in my dismal frame of mind. Then Alaric came in the door having been sent back from the hospital because there was nothing wrong with him. Ha! And they call themselves doctors.

So you can see, I did not have a good day, not at all. By the end of it I was depressed, there's no other word for it. What lay in the future for our family? Death and debt and probably worse things.

I avoided Abigail and Alaric and Anupam and ran quickly to find Griselda again and we dawdled home miserably with each other and with heavy legs. I know in books it's supposed to be a heavy heart but I had heavy legs, there's no getting around it. Stomp, stomp, stomp, down the street, round the corner, across the road, holding onto Griselda's hand very tightly. For more than once that day I felt glad of her hot little squirmy hand.

There was nowhere for me to go but home, the home I had destroyed by accidentally bringing MIMI XXX into our lives. Whether it happened that day or any number of days later, the disaster would happen. I just had to sit and wait for it now – I had neither the energy nor the confidence to do anything else. Ashes in my mouth. I kept my eyes on the ground, at all the dead leaves and pieces of discarded rubbish.

Then stomp stomp stomp up the stairs and through the front door into our living room and BOOM! Like a bomb going off. Griselda and I gasped.

Because there, sitting on the sofa, with the television OFF, was my father, my mother, and the Lego Lady!

chapter twenty

. . . THERE IS REJOICING ON THE HOME
FRONT AND I MAKE A DECISION . . .

My father was BEAMING. He wasn't covered with blood
or even one bruise. He leapt up off the sofa and cried out,
'Girls! Girls!! Come in, come in, and say hallo to Mimi!'

I was speechless. I gazed as Mimi: her lips, her
handbag, her amazing purple gown. It was covered with
sequins. I felt faint with the dazzle of them.

'Hello Mimi,' said Griselda, who does whatever my
father says because she is a goody-goody.

She opened her arms to Mimi with a great smile and
Mimi positively fell into them and I thought she was
going to squash her because I don't know if I mentioned
Mimi is on the large side, you might even say obese.

'Darling!' bawled Mimi through greenish lips into
Griselda's left ear, luckily her slightly deaf one. Even so,
Griselda reeled a little.

'Claudie!' said my mother, 'say hallo to your father's ... er ... friend.'

Mimi waved a ghastly finger at me and said, 'We've met, the naughty girl! I saw her picture in the paper.'

My father assumed a stricken look. 'Oh my God,' he wailed out, and sank onto the sofa, his head in his hands.

He is histrionic, I'm afraid, which means a person who loves a bit of drama. But you could tell he wasn't really upset. But why wasn't he? He should be. Why wasn't Mimi strangling him right at that moment with her large muscular fingers?

'I knew she had to be Norbert's child, you naughty girl!' continued Mimi, waggling those very fingers at me again. 'It's been twenty years since I've seen him, but I knew. What a likeness! Incredible! But as I told you, she pretended she didn't know you – children are such tricksters, aren't they?'

'Claudie is fatal,' said Griselda.

'You didn't out-trick Mimi, though darling, did you?' said Mimi, chortling. 'I just looked your daddy up in the phone book! I knew it wouldn't be under his own name, so I just looked up the old codename Captain Koogle and there it was!'

'Captain Koogle?' said my mother, meaningfully, raising her eyebrows.

We knew Koogle was his nickname, which was the name he used in the telephone book (for business reasons) – but 'Captain'?

'Long story,' muttered my father.

There was a silence. I let my schoolbag fall to the ground with a grave thud.

My father began beaming again. He raised a glass in the air. I noticed suddenly that he and my mother and Mimi all had glasses, and my father was pouring champagne. (He always has a bottle of champagne cold and ready in the fridge because you never know.)

'Come here, girls, we're drinking to the future. Our future!'

I had already been through too many shocks that day. I said blankly, 'What future?'

'Our business future!' replied my father grandly. 'All is saved! We're back on track! We're going into business with Mimi!' And he gave her a coy look, if you know what that is. If you don't, you're lucky.

'Oh,' I said. I stared at Mimi in disbelief. Business? 'What sort of business?' I asked.

'The seed business!' my father burst out, as though it was the cleverest idea in the world. He threw an arm around my mother's shoulders and gave her a big squeeze. She had a really very complacent smile on her face.

'Oh,' I said again, struggling to understand.

They clinked glasses. Griselda shouted 'Hooray!', hopped over and sat on my mother's lap. They all looked at me, waiting.

Seeds. So this is what it had come to. Seeds.

'Congratulations,' I said at last. I bowed my head.

Now I understood. At least, I understood what I'd misunderstood. I'd got the wrong end of Mimi. All right –

the totally wrong end. Mimi was not my father's enemy. What had my mother called her – 'your father's ... er ... friend?' That meant only one thing. As I think I mentioned before, my father is very passionate, and he has a lot of old girlfriends. Hard as it was to believe, Mimi was one of them.

She hadn't been looking for him to kill him at all. She just wanted to go into business with him. I suppose having emerged from the hill country she was looking around for something to do when she saw my photo in the paper. Poor Mimi. That's fate for you. Now she was going to hand over money to my father to pay off those debts that kept him inside breathing deeply, and jump on the bus with Griselda and my mother, selling seeds. How on earth had he talked her into it? I shook my head. Poor, stupid Mimi. Twenty years of safety in the hill country, only to meet up again with Norbert.

'Come on, Claudie!' My father tossed down a glass of champagne. 'Cheer up! Didn't you hear what I said? It's all over. Everything's going to be all right now – in fact, everything's absolutely wonderful.'

'Have a lollipop, you little darling,' said Mimi, reaching into her handbag. From its depths, she produced something on a stick that looked like it had been there a long, long time. She was actually talking to Griselda but I took it because of the laws of primogeniture, and Griselda cried so Mimi produced another one, even mouldier than the last.

'I love sweet things, don't you! Those lovely sweeties you made for me last time, darling,' Mimi went on in a gurgle. 'They were wonderful! Scoffed the lot – couldn't help myself!!'

My Cornflake kisses – surely not! She didn't mean them! But I remembered the teacups – of course! And the empty plate. Oh, how stupid I had been – how vain my struggles! Mimi must have come round while I was out, and my father had let her in quite happily. I suppose he just hadn't mentioned it to me until he was sure she was going to give him the money. In some matters, my father can be remarkably cautious.

Griselda and I sucked on our lollipops. Mimi and my mother and father got all noisy and laughing and turned on some music and my mother got out her seed catalogues to show them to Mimi and Mimi thought they were just FASCINATING and what about the BULBS?

I could see where that was heading. I swallowed the remains of my antique lollipop and turned my back on them all and went to my room. I locked the door.

I lay down on the bed. I looked up at the ceiling and closed my eyes. I forced myself to become calm. Gaggles of laughter were coming from the living room. I would not get upset.

Now you may think, after all I'd been through, all the mistakes I'd made, I'd be a Spent Force. You may in particular think that I'd abandoned my ambition to serve literature and become a Baroness. But that was far from the truth, believe me. If anything, I was more viciously ambitious than ever. Especially now my entire family had given themselves up to seeds.

I am persistent, you see. I am persistent and I am resilient, which means you can recover from deadly diseases one after the other and rise up stronger every time. I would rise again, I would succeed. I would serve literature and be made a Baroness and sit in the House of Lords even though I would be a Lady. Nothing would stop me – nothing! Not Mimi, not Griselda, not even Leo or Cinnamon – I would trample them all before me in my race to the top.

Because I had a new idea. Remember how the Editor said to me, 'Write from LIFE!'

Well, that's what I would do. I'd write from LIFE. In particular, MY life.

I pulled out an exercise book from under the corner of the bookshelf where I'd wedged it to stop it from rocking. It was an old maths book – only a few pages had been used, so I ripped them out and sat up at my desk, sucking on my pencil.

I thought very hard about my life, and where I should start my book. I thought about the things that had happened to me as far back as I could remember (which wasn't much) and then I thought about the things that had happened to me in the past few days (which was a lot). I thought and I thought and then I thought, well, I could spend all night thinking, I'd better get writing. I started with the sentence that began all my troubles.

I wrote: 'My father is not a comedian.'

My father banged on the door. 'CLAUDIE!' he shouted, sounding just like Griselda, except that he is a man.

'Come on out, Claudie! We're missing you.'

I could have said, 'I am in a state of sublime com-position', but my father is not an artist so he wouldn't understand. I looked down at the page. You can't rush inspiration. It was probably time for a rest.

I unlocked the door and went out to the living room where they were eating corn chips and Griselda was singing 'There were Ten in the Bed' to Mimi except she was singing 'There were one hundred and fifty-two in the Bed' because she is not very good at numbers over four. My father was smiling fondly at her and my mother was calmly reading a seed catalogue, so everyone was happy in their own simple way, I suppose.

Mimi gave me a poke in the ribs. 'What a hoot!' she said, although what exactly she was referring to I still don't know.

I sat down next to her on the sofa, but not too close. Her sequins looked dangerous. It was strange, having her in the living room like one of us, after I'd spent so much time thinking of her as a murderous maniac. I could get used to her, I suppose. Well, you can get used to anything.

I looked at my father, grinning there, and sighed. What kind of a human being is this? I remembered a story he told me once, about a man who is being chased by a tiger. The man runs and runs and the tiger is after him, and he falls over a cliff, but he manages to hang on to a little scrap of rock that stops him from tumbling down to his death. But the tiger is snarling down at him with its great big horrible teeth crawling closer and closer and the scrap of rock starts to crumble and he's going to fall into the sea and be killed! Then the man suddenly notices a beautiful red flower growing on the cliff's edge just near his nose, the most beautiful flower he's ever seen, and he thinks, Well, isn't that lucky! And he stops thinking about the tiger above and the ocean below and the crumbling cliff and he just thinks how nice the flower is and how much he is enjoying himself.

Well, that's my dad, I'm afraid.

He leaned over and put his head on my shoulder like a puppy and said, 'Here's to the beautiful face that saved us all!' because of my photograph in the local paper, of course, and it was his joke because everyone knows I look just like him.

But I can take a joke, even a weak one. I accepted the glass of sarsparilla that Mimi was offering me, though it is a drink I particularly dislike, and I smiled back at him. Perhaps I even laughed a little bit, to be encouraging.

You have to remember, after all, that my father is not a comedian.